Gun Dog

PETER LANCETT

Ransom

Gun Dog

PETER LANCETT

Series Editor: Peter Lancett

Published by Ransom Publishing Ltd.
51 Southgate Street, Winchester, Hampshire SO23 9EH, UK
www.ransom.co.uk

ISBN 978 184167 713 2

First published in 2009
Copyright © 2009 Ransom Publishing Ltd.
Cover by Flame Design, Cape Town, South Africa

*This work is humbly
dedicated to the memory of:*

*Lieutenant Colonel, USAF,
Virgil 'Gus' Ivan Grissom*

*Lieutenant Colonel, USAF,
Edward Higgins White II*

*Lieutenant Commander, USN,
Roger Bruce Chaffee*

27th January, 1967

*Those of us who still remember,
weep at your loss as we marvel at
your courage. Godspeed you all.*

CHAPTER 1
Bad timing

It's all over the news again, in the papers and on television. Another kid has been shot dead, so it's all grieving parents telling us how little Billy was such a good boy and all. Telling us how little Billy only played football and was never involved in any trouble. Yeah, sure.

And of course the police are going to be moving heaven and earth, leaving no stone unturned. Yeah, right.

We've heard it all before. And there's the usual bunch of quotes from friends and neighbours. There they are, telling us what a nice neighbourhood it is and how shocking it all is and how they can't believe that it's happened right on their doorsteps. And of course, Princess Diana Syndrome has kicked in; you know, the bunches of flowers as close to the scene of the tragedy as the police will let them get. Mostly they're placed there by people who never even knew little Billy. It's on the telly, right, so everybody wants to be a part of it. What a bloody country this is.

And the reason I'm thinking about this now, while I'm riding home on my beaten-up BMX, is because I'm feeling the weight of what's in the canvas bag strapped to my back. It's books, mostly – as you'd expect, with me coming home from the library and all – but it's the other thing that's in there that puts the pressure on my mind. It's the gun.

Bad timing. It's bad timing that put the gun there. They say that timing is everything. I read that all the time. Well I got my timing all wrong, staying late at the library like that. Late, so that it's near dark when I turn onto the estate where I live. Late as I notice, as always, the line of young trees planted alongside the road that have been stripped or pulled out, the remains of some pathetic attempt by the council to make our area look nicer. Late as I notice, as always, the casual rubbish and the broken glass in the gutters. And inevitably, I notice the cans. Wherever you see the cans, you can pretty much picture the loose gangs of kids around my age and younger, even, wearing Burberry caps like it's standard issue uniform or something. You can hear them swearing, drinking, shouting, chucking stuff about. The kind of casual loutish behaviour that makes the rest of us feel uncomfortable... makes us cross over the road, walk quicker, head down, no eye contact. But, hey, I'm not judging them, I come from these streets just like they do. The estate is a mass of red brick semi-detached houses built in the fifties. A land fit for heroes is what my teacher says they were trying to build. Bet they never envisaged just how the children of heroes would turn out.

So anyway, like I say, I'm riding home from the library, and I'm deep into the estate. I see them, of course, as I approach the boarded-up old pub, the Heart of Oak. There are about seven or eight of them, boys that I know from the estate and from school. And I see the uniform of Burberry and the hooded sweatshirts and trainers and track-pants and they're fooling around and spilling into the road. There's a lot of shouting and swearing and raucous humourless laughter. I hear a bottle smash. And one of them is pissing up against the wall of the pub. Right there in plain sight, with the street-lamp like a stage spotlight giving him a moment of fame. Chavs like these are part of the local furniture here where I live. They're not friends. And I'm riding on the other side of the road and I'm sure as hell not going to look over at them. As often as not that's all it will take for them to feel affronted and offended. And then it *would* be time to be afraid. So I'm just going to ride on by.

'Hey Davies, over here.'

I hear the words just as I see him step out into the road and point at me. Roddy Thompson is a big lad and boasts three

Anti-Social Behaviour Orders or ASBOs as they're commonly known. Dreamt up I reckon by some arrogant prat who lives in wealthy and isolated splendour with no idea how the rest of us actually live. Do they really think an ASBO, regarded as a badge of honour by the rest of the crew, could possibly be the answer? And just take a look at Roddy Thompson – do you think he fears one of those orders for one second? Yeah, right.

I bet you're wondering why I don't just pedal hard and get the hell away. Well if you're wondering that, then it's obvious you've never even *been* to an estate like mine, much less lived on one. And just where are you going to run to? So, swallowing back the pulse of fear-driven vomit that's leapt into my throat, I turn my bike towards big Roddy and coast to a halt right in front of where he's standing.

Big Roddy grips hold of the handlebars of my bike, but even he must know that I'm not going anywhere until he's finished with me. I see the letters that he's tattooed himself onto the fingers of his hand. I saw this old film once, and there was this ancient actor who had 'love' and 'hate' tattooed on his fingers, and I guess that must have been shocking, back then. Roddy has the letters K – U – C – F on the fingers that I'm looking at. I'll leave you to work out the actual word that he spelled. Probably the only word that he *can* spell.

'Where are you goin' Davies?'

'Just home.' I look beyond Roddy and the two or three others that have gathered around too close for my liking. In the dark shadows in an alcove in the far wall of the pub, I can see Sammy Williams. And someone else. A girl. Sammy has his back to me, but I know it's him. The girl I don't recognise, because she's beyond him and her back is pressed against the dark bricks. It's obvious to me, and to anyone else passing by, that they are having casual and brutal sex. Right there in the open. Like dogs.

Others of this little gang have surrounded me now. They're not saying anything but they stand very close, invading my space. It's uncomfortable, but I say nothing. I feel one of them tugging at the canvas bag strapped to my back. It's like he's pulling on it or leaning on it, so that I sag and have to brace myself against being pushed to the ground.

'What's in the bag?'

I turn my head, but can't work out which of the grinning louts has spoken.

'Just books.'

Even I can hear the little quiver of fear in my voice. I'd wanted to sound cool because they'll sense the slightest hint of fear like wild animals do. I've blown it.

'What do you want books for, you ponce? You think it *makes* you something?'

Snarled words from behind me again. A push at the bag on my back, so that I nearly fall over, bike and all. Roddy, gripping tight to the handlebars, holds it steady.

'No, no – I just…'

'You just think that school shit is going to get you somewhere.'

I'm looking at Roddy and he's looking past me to the kids behind as he speaks. I feel the pressure on my canvas bag loosen up. I'm standing straight. And I'm shaking, right? I'm scared now and no point hiding it. They could probably see *that* from space. I don't answer, just look past Roddy. I don't want to look anyone in the eye. Beyond Roddy I can see Sammy Williams starting to walk towards us. He has the dead eyes of a shark, but he doesn't move as smoothly. He's shuffling, stoop-shouldered and slack-jawed. Without a care in the world, he's wiping his dick on the *Nike* track pants he's wearing, then tucking it away. He doesn't care who's seen. Behind him, the girl is making a half-hearted effort to smooth down a short skirt. I don't recognise her, but then I'm not looking at her face. If she was ever wearing anything under that skirt before, she's making no effort to do so now. I've seen everything. And she's seen me looking, but she doesn't care. I've seen enough of her to notice that she's nothing special.

Over-heavy make-up and hair pulled back tight in a 'Croydon face-lift'. Maybe she could be really pretty, but you couldn't really say with her looking as she does now. Sammy is right up behind Roddy and the girl is standing just behind Sammy and to one side. I feel like I'm on stage and that all eyes are upon me. I look up at Roddy and he must see that I am scared shitless, because he just grins and shakes his head.

'Nah, that school crap won't make you something. But this will.'

Roddy reaches inside his navy blue zip-up hooded sweatshirt… and I see three small patches sewn onto the arm as it flashes across, close to my face. ASBO ASBO ASBO – one for each of the three he's been given; a neat piss-take. But I'm not going to smile at it. It's all I can do not to whimper with fear. I'm expecting a knife – they all carry knives and they're all happy to use them. My eyes must be wide and wild and I can smell the cigarette smoke, the spliff smoke. I hear the rattle of a can in the gutter behind me.

And then there is Roddy's hand, right in front of my face. And it's not holding a knife at all. It's holding a gun. I must just gasp out loud because they're all laughing at me.

'This will make you something. This is what counts around here.'

He says this like we're standing in South Central Los Angeles or the Bronx in New York or something. But we're on a council estate in England. Since when did you have to have a gun to amount to something in a place like this?

I'm focused on the blue-black metal, shiny like there's a fine film of oil coating it. And the black rubber hand grip. Roddy points it right in my face.

'This could blow your head right off.'

He's not laughing as he says this. I'm not laughing either. Especially when he leans beyond me, and I feel my bag open and feel something being dropped inside. I know what that something is. Roddy has his hands on my shoulders. He's looking me right in the eye, so that I have to look down.

'I want you to keep that for me for a while – don't mind, do you?' He sneers, all sarky. And I'm shaking my head even as I'm trembling. He seems happy with that reaction.

'That's good. Tell you what; you can have her if you want.' He turns his head and indicates the girl with the Croydon face-lift standing behind Sammy. I look up and see her taking a long drag from a cigarette and blowing the smoke out of her nostrils.

She notices me, but I look away because, to tell the truth, I'm embarrassed as much as I'm afraid.

'Go on, you can have her. We all have.'

I shake my head, I just want to go.

'Suit yourself. But look after that thing in your bag now. It will only be for a couple of days. Keep it safe.'

And then there's clear road in front of me and no hands holding my bike. So I pedal, but not fast, not like I'm running away. Even though I am. Behind me I hear something said and I don't quite catch the words. But then the girl's screeching voice is following me down the road and catching me, surrounding me.

'Ain't I good enough for you or summfin?'

She shouts a lot more but I'm not going to repeat those words.

So here I am, turning into my road, not far from my house. And like I say, the canvas bag on my back weighs heavier and heavier. I'm more alert than I've ever been and I notice the rubbish in the streets, the houses with well-tended gardens, and the ones where no one has cared. And, although it's a pleasant enough evening, I wonder that there are no people about on the streets or in those gardens. And I can't help thinking of Roddy holding that gun so close to my face. Roddy Thompson is fifteen years old. And a year behind me at school.

I want to break free

I'm off the bike, manoeuvring it so that the front wheel pushes open the garden gate on its squeak-free hinges. Dad sees to that. It's on a spring too, so it bangs closed behind me.

It's awkward to do, but I take the trouble to put my bike into the shed and snap the padlock shut. I just simply know that if I leave it in the backyard, even though it's hidden from the street, it probably won't be there in the morning. I know where I live, and while I'm not ashamed of it, I'm far from being proud of it.

I'm holding my canvas bag in one hand. If I look down at it, I fancy I can see the bulge made by the gun. Maybe I'm imagining that, but I twist the bag in my hand just the same so that the bulge is tucked inwards, facing me. It's better to think about the books in that bag; stuff that I need to help me with a couple of school assignments.

Yeah, I'm not proud of this place and I want to get the hell out as soon as I can. And while those kids might be right, and reading books doesn't *make me something*, I know that books will set me free. I have just one goal, and that's university. One far from here I'm hoping, and I don't care how much debt I rack up in student loans. I just want to be somewhere else.

The back door is unlocked and I step into the kitchen. Mum is at the sink, washing dishes. She smiles at me and looks down at the bag swinging against my thigh.

'Been to the library again? I guessed as much. Your tea is in the microwave. Want me to warm it up?'

She's worked in a supermarket all day and she's come home and cooked for the four of us, and now she's doing the dishes and she still has time to smile. The thing is, she's as proud as anything that I'm turning out right. Well, what I let her see of me is, at any rate. I think that she wants my university dream as much as I do. I'm surprised, really, because she's already had a success to boast about. My sister is in her final year at the University of Sussex in Brighton. She's reading Law and she's doing really well. She doesn't come home often, not even in the holidays.

It's not likely that my kid brother is going to be academically inclined though. He's fourteen and he hates school. He stays away as often as not. He screens it from Mum pretty well, although of course *I* know the days when he's not there. I'd never say anything, and he knows that. We get on OK, him and me. But we don't hang around together. He has his friends. I have mine. And, anyway, most of the time I want to get on with my school work. I want to be able to choose which university I go to. I keep thinking of Brighton, where Catherine is now. I like the idea of being by the seaside. And it won't be awkward or anything; she'll be gone by the time my turn comes around.

I look at the microwave and I can smell that it's a slice of meat pie in there. I'm a sucker for Mum's meat pie.

'Yeah, warm it up. I'm just going to take these to my room. I'll be down in a minute.'

I don't even blink, I don't even concern myself with what's in the bag. Mum was never going to ask me to tip out the contents on the kitchen table. I think that she's naïve about what goes on in the streets outside. Probably just as well. I think that I should help her more, talk to her more. But I never do. I just let her cook and clean and work for me. Not *just* for me. But you know what I mean.

I wander into the living room on my way to the stairs. Dad is asleep in his chair, facing the television. The local news is on and I just about make out the fuzzy images of cars being raced around the streets of an estate pretty much like mine. Might even *be* mine. This is a big estate after all. It's going to be a story about anti-social kids but I don't stop to look and listen. I leave Dad to his slumber with the cup of tea going cold on the little wooden table beside his chair. Dad works hard too, as an electrician, and he's doing lots of overtime at the moment.

I take the stairs two at a time. I can already hear the noise of a shoot 'em up video game. That will be my brother in his room. I hear the screeching of tyres and the gunshots and behind it all the thump thump rhythm of the hip-hop music. I like hip-hop and R&B, but I couldn't work with it booming right in my ear. If there's one person in this house who would be impressed rather than appalled by what I have in my bag, it would be Sean. He's not a bad kid, I think, but he's into street culture. On the video console, he's Gangsta Number One, but in real life he doesn't run with the roughest kids on the estate. I don't think he does. It's at times like this that I'm glad that Catherine has gone and we each have our own room. Like I said, I'd never be able to study with that row going on.

On the landing at the top of the stairs, I step past Sean's room and push open the door to my own.

'Yo, Stevie!'

Sean talks like he's Jay-Z or something. I don't understand how he knows I'm here with all the noise from his dumb game. Now his face is round the door jamb, grinning.

'Been waiting for ya bro. Wanna race some? Wanna get thrashed?'

I shake my bag at him and I know that books are the same to him as garlic to a vampire.

'Maybe later. I have some work to do first.'

'Yo's wasting yo life, bro.'

He's gone and his door is shut behind him before I can reply and really, to tell the truth, I'm glad. In my room I take the books out of my bag and lay them on my bed. I leave the gun in there. Where am I going to hide it? If this was a movie, I'd have a lockable metal box in which I keep my diary, or some such shit. But this is real and I don't keep a diary. The solution is much simpler than it would be in any movie. My bed is in a corner of my room and butts up to two walls. I'm just going to put that gun in a plastic bag and shove it right into the corner, under my bed. No one will ever find it there. And it is only for a day or so.

I don't normally throw the bolt on my door, but that's exactly what I do now. Because in truth, now I'm safely here in my room, the gun is beginning to fascinate me. I take it out of the canvas bag and I weigh it in my hand and just look at it. I turn it over, I feel its weight. I smell it. The gun oil is somehow sweet. I fancy that I'm smelling for gunshot residue like on CSI, but I wouldn't recognise it even if it was present. It's terrible to admit this, but I'm even wondering if it's been fired. I'm sure that it must have been. And I wonder if anyone has been shot with this particular gun.

I sit at my computer with the gun on my lap. I'm surfing the net because I want to know what type of gun it is. How crazy is that? Actually, I find it quite quickly on an American gun dealer's website. I hold the gun in front of me and compare it with the picture on the screen. No question about it, I'm holding a Ruger P95 9mm automatic. And I discover that it carries a fifteen round magazine. I'm becoming quite the expert, in just a few minutes.

The gun is held in two hands, the way I've seen them hold handguns on television and in the movies. I'm squinting down the gunsight along the top of the barrel, and the strange thing is, I do feel powerful holding it and pointing it.

Bang bang bang on my door.

'Steven, your tea's ready.'

I swear that I squeal and the gun skitters out of my hands and clatters to the floor beneath my desk.

'Yeah, I'll be right down.'

I hope my voice isn't too muffled. I don't want Mum trying the door and wondering why it's bolted. I find the fallen gun and now I wrap it in a plastic bag. I can feel my heart racing as I squirm under the bed and push the package into the far corner. I run my fingers through my hair to straighten it before unbolting my door and heading – still trembling with shock – for the stairs. Bloody guns.

CHAPTER 3

You wouldn't want to be a teacher

I'm at school. I'm sitting in a classroom next to my best friend Andy Hartnell. It's geography; not my favourite subject, but it's OK. And the teacher is Ms Augustine, and you know what? I'll admit this – I quite fancy her. She's in her late twenties, I'd say, and she has this long blonde hair that she sometimes wears in a pony tail – like today. And she smiles a lot, which is when I fancy her the most.

This class is pretty well behaved, I'd say. I mean there's talking and fooling around, and passing notes and throwing paper at each other. But none of it is malicious. And when Ms Augustine turns round and asks for quiet, well, she actually gets it. For a little while at least. I know from what I read in the papers that older people would say that even this class is out of control, but I can tell you what it's like in classes where they just don't give a damn. There are classes in this very school where kids are walking around, swearing at each other, shouting across at each other, and even fighting. Not all the time, but it goes on. I'm just glad I don't have any classes like that. I mean, what chance have you got of learning anything when the kids are just jerking around like that? I know, I know; I'm meant to find that kind of stuff OK. But you might be surprised by how many of us just want to do well enough here so that we can move on. I'm not the only one. University, remember? It's all I think of. And if I can't learn, then I won't get there.

I don't know what I actually want to be when I'm older and out of here. I've thought perhaps of being a lawyer, like Catherine. But really I have no idea. Maybe a journalist. One thing is for sure though. I don't want to be a teacher. I've seen what happens when a teacher tries to take control of a class. You know, like the classes I've just been on about. I've seen the swearing and the abuse. I've seen the taunting. And I've seen the beatings.

This school is actually not so bad. There are schools far worse than this. But let me tell you some of the things that have happened right here, just this year. First off – and I'd like you to understand that this was a class of thirteen and fourteen year olds – there was what happened to Mr Kowalski. He was trying to teach maths through the usual noise and shouting, when one kid got up and walked across the classroom and punched another lad right in the face where he was sitting. Mr Kowalski tried to intervene and told the first boy to get out of the classroom. That sounds like a pathetic response, but it's about all that a teacher can do, no matter what happens. Teachers are not allowed to touch us at all, no matter what. And we all know that too. It's our 'human rights' isn't it? It's the law. A teacher touches any of us and we don't want them to, then it's a quick call to the police and it's the teacher who will end up suspended. We all know that. Teachers and kids alike. Anyway, this boy in Mr Kowalski's class just turned to him and asked who was going to make him get out. And with everyone watching, the boy threw a book that hit Mr Kowalski in the face. Mr Kowalski told him to leave the class once again, but the boy walked right up to him and punched him in the face. Seriously, a thirteen-year-old kid did this. And the boy kept punching and punching, with Mr Kowalski just trying to defend himself and not hitting back, until Mr Kowalski was on the floor. Then the boy just spat on him and walked out. Mr Kowalski never came back after that. But the boy is still here. He was excluded for a week; a week out in the streets and then he was allowed back. I know that this is a true story because my brother Sean is in that class and he was actually there that day.

And like I say, despite such major incidents, this is far from being the worst school in the area. Mostly it's just niggling disruptive behaviour. Sometimes there's a competition to see how quickly you can make this other teacher, Mrs Conway, cry. It can be funny. She's stupid letting herself get upset so easily. But it's enough to make my mind up for me. Nah, I could never be a teacher. Never.

Anyway, back to this class, and there goes the bell. Ms Augustine lives to teach another day. I hang back while the others pour out of the classroom. I hold the door open for Ms Augustine, like I always do, and she smiles and says thank you, like she always does. I don't know what her perfume is, but I do like it.

Now it's break time, so I go outside. There's a place around the back of the school where you can pretty much be certain no teacher is going to disturb you. Why the hell would they want to when they can stay in the staffroom and have a quiet life? So anyway, that's where I head. When I get there, Sammy Williams is there with a couple of other boys from his class who I don't really know but recognise. Sammy nods to me and I notice those cold black eyes of his beneath the peak of his Burberry cap. I nod back and reach into the inside pocket of my jacket. I take out a packet of cigarettes and silently offer one to Sammy. Sammy shakes his head. I offer one to the two other boys, but one of them pulls his hand from behind his back and waves a huge spliff in front of my nose.

'Wanna try this with us?'

Sammy's voice is low and slow, so it seems like he's tried enough already.

'It's really good skunk.'

I shrug and put my cigarettes away. The boy with the spliff hands it over to me and turns away. It's clear he doesn't want to talk to me. Sammy is holding out a disposable lighter, so I touch the end of the spliff to the flame and suck. The smoke is hot, much hotter than cigarette smoke, but the taste is sweet as I drag it deep into my lungs. It really is good skunk.

Now, normally, I wouldn't expect Sammy Williams to be offering me a smoke of skunk.

We don't exactly mix. On the other hand, we've known each other all our lives. Sammy lives in the next street down from me and his brother was in Catherine's class when she was at this very school. They even went out together for a while. Their paths have parted since. Sammy's brother is in prison. I've told you where Catherine is. But I'm guessing that the real reason that I'm being given more than just the time of day here is because of the favour I'm doing for Big Roddy. Because I'm hiding that gun. And because Sammy knows that I can be trusted to do it.

'You should have had that bird last night.'

I'm passing the spliff to the boy who had given it to me, so I have to turn to Sammy.

'She was well up for it. We all had her. Some of us more than once.'

Sammy is grinning beneath his dead eyes so that it's clear that he certainly had more than his share.

'Bet she was dripping all the way home.'

One of the other boys sniggers and Sammy sniggers too. Then he starts to laugh.

'Who was she anyway?'

I have to say something, if only to stop that stupid spliff-laughter.

Sammy just shrugs.

'Dunno. Just some slapper who was in the mall next to the station. She wanted to hang, so we let her chill with us so long as she'd screw us all.'

I don't want to ask anything more. It is all too depressing. All the same, I can't help thinking that perhaps I'd missed out. And then our heads all turn at once, towards the school gates, like we've all had some sixth sense experience. The school gates are a couple of hundred yards away and what we can see is an agitated gang of kids around the gates, and then one or two running off in different directions. And most of all we can see the kid who is running towards us.

As this kid gets nearer we can see that it is Rob Harrison. He's a few years younger than us and really far too fat to be comfortable running like this. Pretty soon he's slid to a halt in front of us and he's gasping and wheezing fit to puke. Sammy grabs him and slams him against the wall.

'What's going on?'

Eventually the fat kid is able to blurt out something marginally coherent.

'It's big Roddy Thompson. He's been beat up and stabbed.' He pants, 'They've killed him.'

Sammy still has hold of the kid's jacket lapel and throws him to the ground where he lies, still panting and gasping for breath.

'Bollocks.'

You can tell that Sammy is unsure though, the way he's watching the agitated kids up by the school gate. Next thing, Sammy is making his way up there and the other two boys follow him. I stand where I am and watch them go. On the ground, Rob Harrison is starting to breathe easier.

'It is true you know.'

I look down at him, taking my cigarette packet out of my jacket again. I light a cigarette as the fat kid holds out a hand for me to help him to his feet. I just blank him and walk away like he doesn't exist.

In a way, I sort of know that it *can't* be true, that Big Roddy can't be dead. All the same, I bet you know what I'm thinking about. That's right, the slick black Ruger P95 wrapped in a plastic bag under my bed. Is it mine now? Or will Sammy or any one of the others claim it? I'd have to give it up if one of them asked for it.

I'm no angel as I'm sure you're gathering, but I'm not going to make enemies for no reason. The streets on our estate can be more dangerous than you'd ever imagine. I smile as I wonder what the hell I think I'm going to do with a gun in the first place. It's all stupid anyway. Big Roddy's not dead. It's just rumour. Happens all the time.

I finish my smoke as I walk back to the main school building. The rest of the day is just going to drag, I know. I just want to get home to the Ruger.

A lovely boy who wouldn't harm anyone

Big Roddy *is* dead. No point me saying that I can hardly believe it or any of that crap, because I can.

I'm sitting in the living room at home with Mum and Dad and Sean, and all four of us have trays on our laps. We always eat in the living room, watching TV. Anyway, there's a local news programme on the TV and it's all about Big Roddy. I recognise where the cameras are showing us. It's a grey concrete precinct of soulless flats where people live. We call it the Concrete Canyon, and it looks depressing on TV, a jumble of graffiti-covered walls and dark abysmal walkways linking square slabs of dismal apartments. And I know from experience that it's even worse seeing it for real.

This seventies-built ghetto is a few miles from here on the outskirts of the other side of town. I've been there because a girl I liked used to live there. The second time I went to visit her, I had the crap beaten out of me when I was walking to the bus stop to go home. It was dark and I had to go along one of the walkways, and then down an unlit stairwell. That's where they jumped me. They left me bleeding and bruised and they stole my phone and my iPod. I can remember them telling me to steer clear of their turf.

I can also remember Dad phoning the police when I got home. I can remember him going spare when he realised they weren't going to send a car around to see us right away. That was when Dad first realised what I or any other kid could have told him ages before; that the police have given up on crime. They don't want to know. They've definitely given up on the streets in estates like ours. And they'd never venture into the desolate Concrete Canyon that we're seeing on the screen now, where Big Roddy bled to death.

The blue and white police tape blocking off the exact place where Roddy snuffed it stands out against the grey of the concrete. I'm looking to see if I can spot blood on the paving stones, but the camera is too far away to see properly. What you can see though, is that already there are little bunches of flowers and a couple of stupid cuddly toys. What the hell is it with people, for fuck's sake? What a nation of feeble professional mourners we seem to have become.

Listen, they're interviewing some woman from our estate now.

'He was a lovely boy. He wouldn't harm anyone. He had his whole life ahead of him.'

Other women standing nearby are nodding their agreement.

'He was a bit cheeky, like, but he wasn't a bad lad. I hope they catch who did it and lock them away forever.'

'I used to work with his mum, like. I don't know how she'll cope with this.'

This interview is taking place outside Roddy's house, but these aren't family members. I'm guessing that they're neighbours just dying to be on TV. And of course they live close by, so they won't let the truth intrude upon their words.

He was a bit cheeky, like, but he wasn't a bad lad. Christ almighty, these are neighbours so they just had to have known! Big Roddy was a loutish, violent, cunning, dirty bastard who would piss on their cars and carried three ASBOs on his sleeve like sergeant's stripes.

'Ha ha ha ha ha – what a load of bullshit!' Sean's only saying what I'm thinking.

'Show a bit of respect – the lad's dead.'

Sometimes I think that Dad is stuck in a time warp. Who cares that an asshole like Roddy Thompson is dead? Lucky for us that we live at this end of this particular street.

It's not so bad here and we're fortunate that groups of kids haven't chosen to hang out here. Probably because we're a well lit and relatively busy road. Dad might not be so respectful if Roddy and his friends had been spending their nights outside our front gate. Bad enough that, even as it is, he has to clear up empty fast food cartons and sweet wrappers and plastic drink bottles and stuff from the garden from time to time.

'I feel sorry for his poor mother.'

Jeez Mum, get real. This woman is a foul-mouthed drunk who will pup out a replacement bastard in no time.

I've finished my tea, so I get up and take my tray into the kitchen. I even think that I could wash my plate, even as I'm putting it in the sink. But I don't wash it of course; Mum will do the dishes later.

I go up to my room. While I'm waiting for my computer to boot, I'm thinking about the gun under my bed. For some reason, it seems kind of disrespectful to want to hold it so soon after Roddy has been killed. It's a stupid thing to say, I know. But all the same, I leave it where it is.

I have homework to do. Something I have to write about King Lear. Actually, I quite like Shakespeare. Once you get behind the poncey language, the stories are really quite good. Ms McNeil who teaches us English has handed out these books with the story of King Lear written in dumb stupid language so that we'll understand it. I'd find it insulting if I stopped to think about it. But the thing is, it means that anything we have to write for this class can be kept simple. Suits my lazy streak, I have to say. Anyway, I want to get this done and out of the way. It's Friday and Andy's coming around later and we're going out somewhere. Dunno where yet. I'll wait and I'll see what he suggests. We'll probably end up going to see a film though. He's been going on about this new Jason Bourne film for ages. Wonder what type of gun Jason Bourne uses?

CHAPTER 5

It's a jungle out there

It's not yet dark and I'm out on the street just outside my house with Andy. I was right – about him wanting to go see the latest Jason Bourne movie that is. It means a trip to the retail park on the far side of town and a visit to the multiplex, and it means spending money. But that's OK; I want to see this movie too. It's funny, but it's like I'm going to be taking a professional interest. As though, now I'm hiding the Ruger, I have something in common with Jason Bourne. Well actually, now I think of it, it's not funny at all. Just weird. Forget that thought. Thank goodness I resisted the mad urge I had to bring the Ruger with me.

We have to walk a fair way to the bus stop. But we can take a short cut through The Gardens – an area of shrubs and trees and grass with a square playground area of red shale in the middle. Sounds lovely, doesn't it? It isn't.

We have loads of time. So we're not in any rush as we slouch down the street with our hands in our pockets.

'Did you hear what happened to Roddy Thompson?'

I look at Andy and I shrug.

'Sure I heard. It was even on the news earlier.'

'Who do you think did it?'

I shrug again.

'Dunno. Could have been anyone over there.'

I'm thinking of the gang of hoodies in

that dark stairwell who robbed me and kicked my head in.

'Yeah. It's pretty grim over there.'

I turn to look at Andy when he says this. After all, here where we live it's hardly Mayfair.

Andy realises what he's said and smiles sheepishly.

'Well, compared to here it's grim. You have to admit that.'

And he's right; I do have to admit that.

We continue our slouching walk for a while, crossing the intersections of streets that lead off our road. The street signs are unreadable, covered with multi-coloured graffiti. We see the same indecipherable tags everywhere; on walls, on garage doors, on the post box that we pass. It's like the way that dogs piss to mark out their territory. I hate it, but what can I do?

The gutters at the edge of the road are filled with fast food cartons, wrappers and plastic bottles and cans. Every now and then there is broken glass. And you have to watch where you're treading because there's dog shit on the pavement too.

Even some of the rubbish has a tired look to it. Plastic and polystyrene ripped and torn and grey with dust and dirt, and flattened where it's been trodden and trampled and run over. It makes the place feel even seedier and more run-down. It just shows how infrequently the council sends road cleaners around here. Wonder if they appear more often where the councillors actually live? Dad says that there's never any money for anything any more, except there always seems to be plenty for councillors' pay and expenses and index-linked pensions. And jobs that nobody really understands like 'Diversity Co-ordinators' and 'Five-a-day Co-ordinators'. This last bunch apparently has to make sure that everyone has five portions of fruit and veg a day. Some days I definitely don't have five portions of fruit and veg, but no one has ever cautioned me about it. Except maybe Mum. And she definitely doesn't work for the council. Dad gets really angry about stuff like this, he's always going on about the way things were, but I can just accept that it's the way that things are. I've never known it to be any different.

We pass a wide street as we head towards The Gardens. On the corner of this street, on the opposite side of the road to us, is a piece of flat gravel-covered ground with a couple of old concrete garages. The doors of one of the garages have been kicked in and burned. The other one has peeling paint and a broken grimy window. In front of this garage is a car. It's a clean and tidy car, even if it is ten years old. A Nissan Micra. It belongs to the couple who live in the house on the corner next to this piece of ground, Mr and Mrs Allen. I know this, because to me and my brother and sister, they aren't Mr and Mrs Allen – they're Uncle Jack and Aunty Margaret. Not that they are really relatives, just that we've always called them that. Aunty Margaret has looked after all three of us during school holidays while Mum was at work. Before that, she even looked after our mum, while *her* mum went to work. They've looked after quite a few kids round here. They are in their seventies now, but they still look after their house and garden, and I know that the little car is their pride and joy. They bought it brand new the day after Uncle Jack retired. I've been out in it with them many times as a little kid, squeezed into the back seat and listening to kid-crap songs on the cassette that Aunty Margaret used to keep in the glove compartment. Happy times, I guess.

A thump, the sound of rock on metal, makes Andy and me turn our heads. There are two kids using the little Nissan as cover, and from behind the burned out garage three other kids are gathering rocks to throw at them. I recognise all these kids. They are about ten and eleven years old. The two hiding behind the car are laughing as the rocks come flying at them. All I can think is that the poor little car is going to be scratched and dented. Maybe worse.

A rock goes way beyond the car and smashes against the red brick wall of the house. I feel that I should do something, put a stop to this before there is serious damage, but the fact is I do nothing. I just watch it all going on as I walk on by. You just can't afford to get involved in anything like this; everyone knows that. And one of the three bastards behind the garage I recognise. It's Derek Rogers, and the Rogers family are trouble. There seem to be loads of them living in a house that they've made squalid even by the unkempt standards of a lot of the houses on this estate. And they are criminals. Every foul-mouthed stinking one of them. They are noisy, drunken, and clannish to a degree you can barely imagine. To even look askance at one of them is to challenge the whole rotten pack. The mother alone has been inside a few times in the past for theft and the fat ugly sow of a woman sports more tattoos than a San Quentin lifer. The kids all look the same, and they have these slitty eyes so that you can't help feeling that there's some inbreeding going on. Doesn't bear thinking about. It's just like that film, *Deliverance*. Needless to say, disorderly conduct is not a criminal charge to this lot; it's a lifestyle choice. Do I even have to mention that they are brutal and violent? So, however much it's breaking my heart to see these little scumbags hurting Uncle Jack and Aunty Margaret's car like that, my cowardly instinct for self-preservation has won over. I feel sick and I want to cry. I'm not kidding.

What makes it all worse somehow is the knowledge that it's not personal. Not yet. These kids have nothing against Uncle Jack and Aunty Margaret. It's just unfortunate that this is where their selfish thoughtless anti-social stupid game has brought them. So you really ought to be able to just tell them to clear off, right? What should it matter where they go to make their mischief? But what is really terrible is that it *will* get personal if Uncle Jack and Aunty Margaret step outside to remonstrate with them. I'm praying that they don't. I'm really praying hard. For their sake.

I notice the curtains twitch. Please don't come out, please don't come out. Uncle Jack and Aunty Margaret don't realise that it's a jungle out there. Another clang of rock against metal. I look to where the rock has come from and Derek Rogers is looking right at me.

'What the fuck are you looking at?'

I'm not going to answer that whatever you might think of me, and neither is Andy. Next thing you know, Rogers and the kids with him are hurling rocks over at us. And we're putting our arms up as shields and we're running as the foul language and bricks follow us down the road, unmindful of the couple of cars that pass in both directions. These drivers must be local; they know better than to stop. Then soon enough we've left the foul kids and the rocks behind and we're turning into The Gardens. Rogers and the goblins that trail around with him haven't bothered to follow us. I'm in two minds about this. On the one hand, I'm glad that we no longer have to consider them; but on the other hand, I'm wondering if they are still hanging around Uncle Jack and Aunty Magaret's place.

I feel guilty and angry and ashamed all at the same time. I mean, these kids were about ten or eleven years old. Andy and me shouldn't be running from the likes of them. In the natural order of things, they really ought to be wary of us. But the rules on estates like ours don't follow any natural scheme. Remonstrate with kids like that, chase them off the way we ought to be able to and we'd have to watch our backs forever. You think I'm exaggerating? I told you about the Rogers family. Any perceived affront to one of them and you find you're dealing with the whole pack of jackals. If one of the bigger ones were to see you on the street, you'd be praying for the speed of an Olympic champion. But that's not the half of it. There's a better than even chance that the criminally violent father of that festering brood, along with one or two of the older yobs in the family, would be at your house battering on your door before you knew it. And suddenly your whole family is at risk.

But what I think is probably the worst of it is that every aspect of your life would be ruined from that moment on. Like I say, I'm not exaggerating. What would happen is that the whelps from this pack of scum and their hangers-on would more than likely decide to hang out on the streets near to your house. Their foul language, yelling, and generally loutish behaviour would be stressful enough. But there would be the vandalism; the broken windows in the middle of the night; the damage to your car parked in the driveway. They'd be spilling into your garden, ripping out any plants and shrubs. You'd hear them in the middle of the night in your yard and you'd look out of your windows and they'd just look right back up at you and jeer their foul-mouthed, mocking invective. It would be loads of tiny little things. But it would be relentless. And they can keep this behaviour going, fuelled by alcohol and drugs, until you eventually break. Trust me, they will never tire of it. They're too stupid to tire of it. And they'll be enjoying it. Don't ever forget that.

So why not just call the police? Ha ha ha. Let's not even go there. Life's too short.

Still, Andy and me, we've got a movie to see so we just keep walking, along the path and through The Gardens. Like I've said, it's getting dark now, but we're not worried about walking through here. And besides, we'd have to walk about half a mile more if we didn't.

'Be good if somebody would just take the Rogers family out, wouldn't it?'

I think about this before I answer. I'm still unhappy with myself, to tell you the truth.

'You'd think they'd have enough enemies, wouldn't you?'

Andy doesn't comment and we continue our unhurried trudge through The Gardens. We're way out of sight of the roads now, and it's getting even darker. As we round a corner, we can see the playground area off to our left. The slides and the swings and the climbing frames are brooding in the shadows like the skeleton frames of dinosaurs in the Natural History Museum. It's way too late for mums and toddlers to be here, so there's no laughing and crying and squealing kids; no dreary single mums with their baby buggies, smoking on the benches. But there are a few older boys there, standing on the dark shale. There are about half a dozen of them, slouching around in that slovenly fashion that they must think is cool, and I can see wisps of grey smoke from the cigarettes or spliffs they're smoking, and the red burning tips. We're too far away for me to recognise who they are, but some are wearing the peaked Burberry cap that's like a uniform to them, and the others are wearing dark sweatshirts. The hoods are pulled up so that they don't have faces from where I'm looking. I shiver, because these hooded kids remind me of that time when I was beaten and robbed, not far from where Roddy Thompson bled to death earlier today. Those kids were dressed just like that, although I doubt that this is the same crew.

I can just about hear the murmuring of their voices. Not the drunken loutish bellowing and fooling around you might expect, so I'm sure that they're transacting business. That can only mean drugs or weapons. Skunk, E, speed, heroin, crack, meth and God knows what else. Or it could be a gun that's being traded. You can imagine why I'd think that, right? And yes, my mind slips back home to my room and the plastic bag under my bed, and the cold black Ruger that lies there.

Actually, it's more likely to be drugs than guns. Despite what the newspapers shriek and what the television gets all weepy over, it's not true to say that there's an epidemic of guns out on the streets. You read the papers and you'd think that every kid either has a gun or could get one cheaply in minutes if needed, but the truth is that guns are still hard to come by for most people. If you're a member of a crew and your crew is part of the drug distribution chain, it's possible that one can be borrowed if a little frightening or enforcing is necessary. Anyone who wants to be tooled up will carry a blade though. Knives are immediate. It was a knife that did for Roddy Thompson. Maybe it wouldn't have happened if he'd been carrying the Ruger he'd given me to hide.

Suddenly, I realise that the murmuring from the group in the playground has stopped. It's as quiet as the grave. And I realise that I'm looking at them and that all of them are looking at me. Jeez, that was stupid, letting my mind wander like that so that I didn't realise that I was looking over at them. I'm scared now, and feeling prickly as the adrenaline courses through me in preparation.

'What the fuck you lookin' at?'

Fight or flight. I remember it from a science lesson in school. That's what adrenaline prepares you for. That's its job, to give you extra speed and strength and sharpen your reflexes for fight or flight. Well, I don't even have to think. It's flight for me.

I kick off and start to run and Andy is only half a stride behind me. Adrenaline's cool like that; it can pulse into your system in half a heartbeat. Neither me nor Andy say anything. Can't talk, all energy needed for flight. I can see through the gloom like it's daylight and all I can hear is the pounding of our feet on the path, and the pounding of the feet of the boys following us in the distance. No shouting, no foul insults from the gang behind us – they're as intent on catching us as we are on getting away. Christ, this is serious. This is scary. We're running parallel with the trees that line the inside of the railings, the boundary of The Gardens. This is thick privet so that we can only see flickering lights from the cars on the main road beyond. The gate is about three hundred metres away and I'm wondering if we can get out before they catch us.

One thing I do know is that we just have to get out onto the streets, where it's lighter, where there is traffic, where there might be people. Not that I think that any of that would bother this lot if they caught us out there. But they might be inclined to be more restrained and to back off earlier in front of witnesses. In the safe anonymity of the darkness here in The Gardens, who knows what they might be capable of. Roddy Thompson bled to death earlier today. Roddy Thompson. Big Roddy. And this is just me and Andy.

I glance behind, just to see if they're gaining on us, but all I see is Andy still that half a stride behind.

'Just run!'

Andy is right. If you're being pursued, you should never look back. Never. Just keep looking forward, concentrate on escape. Even so, I glance to my left and through the trees and beyond the railings, I can just about see that there is a bus coming up. Suddenly I veer to the left and Andy doesn't question, he just turns to follow me. I throw my hands out in front of me and I'm ripping at thick prickly branches that scratch across my face as I burst through a slight gap in the privet trees uncaring. I grab the railings and haul myself up, and all the while the branches contrive to hold me back. I'm too strong for them though. I can hear them crackle and break and splinter as I swing a foot up to gain purchase on the horizontal wrought-iron top beam, while I grab the spikes to pull myself up. I'm over and dropping to the pavement on the other side in one fluid movement, hearing a tear as a jacket pocket snags on one of those spikes and rips. I hear a heavy thump as Andy lands beside me, rolling involuntarily like a paratrooper.

Fifty metres down the road, the bus is at a stop. One elderly woman is stepping onto it and I'm flying down the pavement, waving my hands in the hope that the driver will see me in his mirrors and wait, even as I hear a thump at the railings behind me, and foul threatening curses burning my ears. I don't turn to look for Andy; I don't turn to see if any of that crew is climbing over after me. I have just one focus. Get to the bus.

My lungs are burning and I can see that the old woman has just waved a bus pass at the driver. Why the bloody hell can't she have paid with a note and needed change? Anything to hold the bus up for a second. I could just about cry, expecting to see the bus doors close with that hydraulic hissing sound. But I'm halfway along the side of the bus now, waving like crazy.

'Wait, wait!'

The scream is mine, and this must be a kind driver because the doors stay open. I almost tumble onto the step and reach into my pocket to fish out my travel card. I flash it at the driver and pile on up to the back of the bus, with Andy panting fit to spew right behind me.

Even before we reach the back seat, we hear the hydraulic hiss as the doors slide shut, and the jerk as the bus pulls into the traffic nearly spills us onto the deck. But we catch the backs of some seats and steady ourselves. We throw ourselves down on the back seat of the bus, panting and unable to speak. But we look at each other and just grin. It's not a grin of happiness though; more of relief.

I'm sweating as I turn to look out of the rear window. I don't know what I'm expecting to see, or even what I want to see. I'm relieved to see nothing. They haven't followed us over the railings. One thing's for sure. I won't be taking any short cuts through The Gardens again.

Chapter 6

Someone to watch over me

Jason Bourne does not carry a Ruger. As a matter of fact, he doesn't have a particular gun at all. He uses whatever happens to come to hand. I realise that it's ridiculous that I should feel somehow disappointed. But the fact is that I do. It's like a little bit of my identity has been sucked into that Ruger and now lies wrapped in a plastic bag shoved far under my bed.

The movie is over and we've spilled out of the multiplex with a load of other people and we're standing just outside, beneath the bright lights. There's a lot of noise – people talking to each other, people jabbering loudly into their mobile phones, the sounds of the adjacent video arcades and cars. Always, there is the sound of cars on the retail park. This is where the dreamers congregate – the lads who spend every penny and every minute on their pitiful little hatchbacks with loud after-market exhausts and under-sill LED lights that glow green and purple and orange and red and blue on the asphalt. Then they come here and park next to each other, to show off in-car entertainment systems that are worth more than the vehicles themselves. Slide-out televisions and boom-boxes and amplifiers and sat-nav and DVD players and speakers that would grace any home entertainment system. These are the sort of kids who watch movies like *Tokyo Drift* and imagine that there is a link between themselves and the movie guys with their tricked-out Skylines and Scooby-Doos and Evos. Delusional. And they know it. They'll never have a Skyline with a fifty-grand engine job and nitrous oxide injectors and stuff. Not coming from around here they won't. But they can spend less money and have exactly the same tricked-out entertainment systems, so that's what they do. And that's their link.

Who's deluded though? Didn't I just say that I've been to see the latest Jason Bourne movie and I'm looking to see what gun he carries? Like I think that because I have a gun under my bed I'm in some way part of the world that Jason Bourne inhabits. At least with that lot and the hot hatchbacks, they dream about emulating a world that actually exists. I'm associating myself with a world of spies and assassins that I'm sure is merely a fantasy. And yet I just called *them* delusional. I should just get rid of that gun.

Actually, it's quite cold this evening. I stick my hands in my pockets as we walk out of the bright lights of the multiplex and the arcades and cross the huge car park that surrounds the complex like an over-sized moat. The car park itself is well lit with pools of orange light cascading down from high grey metal lamps.

'You not going to wave?'

Andy has stopped and is craning his head as though he is scanning the heavens.

I know exactly what he's referring to as I watch him pull stupid faces and wave in grand flourishing gestures. He's making a show for the CCTV cameras. On tall metal poles at regular intervals are the plastic globes containing cameras that can spy on every square inch of the retail park. Andy is right to remind me; it's part of our ritual when we come here. So I wave half-heartedly, even though I'm not really in the mood, before sticking my hands back into my pockets against the cold of the evening.

'Do you think anyone is ever actually watching?'

Andy is hurrying after me now. I stop and wait for him.

'I wouldn't know.'

How can any of us know? In England we're watched by CCTV cameras more than any other people in the supposedly free world. There are more than four million CCTV cameras in Britain, and there's been stuff in the papers that lots of them have zoom lenses and listening devices. They say that during a typical day, you probably turn up on a CCTV camera as many as three hundred times. But I don't know anyone who feels safer or less scared because of this.

'Do you know who actually runs these cameras?'

I shake my head and shrug.

'Could be the people who own the retail park.'

I'm just guessing. It could also be a private security company hired out to monitor the area. It could be the local authority. It could even be the police.

'Do you think they actually work?'

'Depends on what you think they're meant to do.'

'What do you mean?'

I'm surprised that Andy has to ask. He's pretty bright – smarter than me I'd say.

'Well, do you think they're here to keep an eye on what's going on, so that they can spot any criminal activity?'

'You'd think so wouldn't you?'

Andy says that in a way that tells me he doesn't actually think that at all; he's just being provocative. I won't disappoint him.

'What about that girl who was raped behind the carpet place three weeks ago?'

I point at the giant modern warehouse-showroom a couple of car parks away but still looming large and grey through the orange glow of the lighting.

'Right behind there, at about this time of night when there were people about. How come that wasn't spotted?'

'It was. They've got film of the three guys dragging her behind the warehouse.'

I turn to look at Andy, shaking my head. He can't be serious about this.

'Yeah and I bet that's a comfort to the girl. She was only fifteen.'

Even I know that her age shouldn't matter but actually it does. She's only young and this has probably ruined her entire life. But I'm on a roll, so I continue.

'It's not like it was spotted as it actually happened. They only looked at those tapes after the crime had been reported. And you know what? The pictures are too dark and grainy to identify anyone properly. Christ, how often do you hear that?'

'They can't be watching every camera all the time. It was just unlucky.'

'I can see how that will cheer her up. Perhaps you should write and tell her that.'

Andy doesn't answer. We carry on walking, across the huge expanse of car park and between the parked cars towards the bus shelter. But all the time I'm thinking of that girl. And I feel sure that the cameras focused on the businesses on this retail park are the ones that are watched the most.

We are supposed to feel safe having these cameras all over the place. Like the knowledge that there is supposedly someone watching will deter potential wrongdoers from doing wrong. I don't buy that. Most people don't. And I'm sure that the girl who was raped doesn't feel safe any more. If you ask me what *might* deter people from behaving badly, I'd have to say that you couldn't do better than have the physical presence of someone big, wearing a uniform, carrying a heavy stick and backed by some kind of authority. Someone actually there, patrolling. And the mass of cameras in every town centre don't seem to have any effect on the drunken, brawling, puking, pissing crowds that gather to get wasted on Friday and Saturday nights. Not that it's totally restricted to weekends.

We're getting to the far side of the car park now, and the parked cars have started to thin out. From some of these cars we hear the persistent rhythm of techno-trance music from the entertainment systems.

Gathered around the cars in places are groups and gangs I don't know or recognise. They all look the same though and dress the same. And talk the same. Actually, it's like a totally separate language. There's nothing new in this. These lot use street talk that I think is based on the language used by American hip-hop stars – not that I've analysed it or anything, but that's how it sounds to me. My brother Sean talks like this all the time. Others – like Andy and me, for example – don't speak like this. But we understand it readily enough. We're immersed in it and surrounded by it. To the chavs who wear the Burberry and the hooded sweatshirts, it's their language of choice. And because I'm thinking of this right now, I'm stretching my ears to listen to what's being said in the group we're now passing.

'Bo bredrin, wa g'wan?'

'Skeen Kelly Richards init?

'She a right sket, init.'

'She's right blinged up and with Stewart Macca.'

'Macca's solid man, so don't be dissin Kelly.'

'Nah, he a pimp, init.'

'Skeen 'is wheels? Fuckin' wack init?'

And so it goes on, but we're out of earshot already. I know instinctively what they're saying; it translates as something like this:

'I say there, friends, what's going on?'

'Have you seen Kelly Richards?'

'She's an utter slut isn't she?'

'Well, she's dressed to the nines and adorned with a great deal of jewellery, and she is currently escorting Stewart MacCartney.'

'MacCartney is something of a tough fellow, so it would be a good idea *not* to say anything disrespectful about Kelly.'

'I disagree –he's actually nothing better than a common male prostitute.'

'Have you seen the car he currently drives? It's absolutely awful, wouldn't you say?'

OK, I shouldn't make fun like that. But I do get a kick out of doing these little translations when I'm listening in on conversations. And by the way, just so that you know; Kelly Richards *is* a slut.

Going home, we stay on the bus for an extra stop. It means we'll have further to walk to get to our houses, but we don't really want to get off anywhere near The Gardens. Even though we don't speak about it in these terms, it's fair to say that our lives have been changed by that little incident earlier. We'll never use The Gardens as a short cut again. So we'll be having to walk further. We'll be having to walk a route that wouldn't be our first choice. It's little things like this that make life more and more restrictive and more and more uncomfortable and more and more stressful on estates like ours. And nobody seems to want to do anything about it.

And for people like us, for my mum and dad, for Andy's mum and dad, there's nowhere to go. People like us don't have the financial clout to move. I mean, my mum and dad own our house. Although we live on a council estate, they bought the house through the 'right to buy' policy which came in before I was even born. They must have been so proud when they did that. Made them homeowners. They must have thought that it would secure our future and would be an investment for us all. They never speak about that now. And while the papers are full of wondrous stories telling of the house-price miracle that sees properties increasing in value each month by more than the homeowners actually earn, my mum and dad don't talk about it. Nobody would ever want to buy a house on an estate like ours. And even if we could sell it, where would we go? All the nicer places have seen their values rise so that we couldn't even dream of buying there.

There are thousands like us. We're trapped. And nobody wants to look after us on estates where there is just drip after drip after drip of anti-social behaviour so that you end up imprisoned within your own four walls. You end up too depressed to want to venture outside. You just don't want to keep having to face up to it.

I dream of getting out. I dream of university. Nobody in our house ever needs to ask Catherine why she doesn't come home as often as she could. We all of us want to avoid that discussion at all costs. Nobody cares about decent people like my mum and dad and Andy's mum and dad. And Uncle Jack and Aunty Margaret.

Walking back through the darkened streets of our estate, Andy and me are pretty quiet. We're taking a route that doesn't even go past The Gardens. But we don't talk about it. There are streetlights throwing down pools of pale yellow or orange light, but it's not as bright here as it was on the retail park. Property is more important than people is a thought that goes through my head, even though I know it's not as simple as that.

Some of the houses we pass are in darkness, the occupants already gone to bed. From others we get the tinted flicker of television calling us to turn and look. One house that we pass, the curtains haven't been drawn and we can see a man and a woman asleep in each other's arms on the sofa while the television bathes them in shimmering changing colours. I think that this is beautiful and poetic, but I don't say that to Andy. And anyway, just then we hear the squealing and laughter of a couple of young kids who really shouldn't be out on the streets so late, but whose parents just don't give a shit.

And then we round the corner and suddenly it's like we've turned up on a film set. We've heard it before we ever got to see it, of course – all the shouting and the swearing and, as we got nearer and could make out the words, the threats. So as we round the corner, we stop to watch. And what we're looking at is four police cars slung any old how in front of a house. The blue lights are spinning so that it all looks like a big deal and that they've cracked a Columbian drug den, or maybe raided an Al Qaeda bomb factory. Neighbours in various states of night-time attire are out in their gardens and on their doorsteps watching. There's a small group of foul-mouthed yobs pointing and swearing, and being prevented from intruding upon the garden of the house by a couple of our uniformed finest. I'd find this entertaining too, as a rule, in the same way that the neighbours who are silently watching do. But this is all going on outside Uncle Jack and Aunty Margaret's house, and my heart sinks to the point where I feel like I want to be sick. Worse still, the baying yobs are all part of the Rogers clan.

I look beyond the Rogers scum and the blue-flashing police cars, to the patch of ground next to the house. And I have to turn away because I can't bear to gaze for long upon the little Nissan Micra that Uncle Jack and Aunty Margaret had saved so long and so hard to get. You can see the dents all over it, and the front windshield is smashed to fuck. The dents are catastrophic too, like the little Micra has been repeatedly kicked and jumped upon. The lights are all smashed out too.

All of a sudden I get flashes in my mind of being in the back of that car with Uncle Jack driving and Aunty Margaret singing the stupid kid songs and me singing along with her. I can feel the tears welling up in my eyes and I don't know where to turn now. I don't want Andy to see.

All at once the commotion increases. Cops are having to physically restrain the Rogers scum as the front door of the house is opened. I see Uncle Jack step out and he looks old in a way I've never noticed before. This ramrod of a man who had once been a Grenadier Guardsman is stoop-shouldered and withdrawn as he shuffles onto his own immaculate garden path. The foul threats of the Rogers scum are blasting around him, drowning the crackling words of the police car radios. I can't turn away from this, no matter how much it's hurting. And it *is* hurting. Uncle Jack has his head bowed, looking down at the path that I watched him weeding only a few days ago. His face looks grey and tired in the shadows. But not frightened. Uncle Jack is a real man and he does not frighten. But what he does seem is bewildered.

I almost call out when I see the handcuffs. The filth have Uncle Jack handcuffed. He's never committed a crime in the whole of his life. And he's in his mid-seventies for fuck's sake! Yeah – takes a lot of guts to arrest an old man and treat him like that. I'm angry – you bet I am. But what am I going to do? I know only too well that I can't speak out on Uncle Jack's behalf. I bet these brave pigs wouldn't think twice about treating me the same way and I'd be joining him down at the nick. And yet *there* are the Rogers scum, yelling and swearing and threatening. And they are not being arrested.

Uncle Jack gets to the garden gate, and

some tiny slip of a woman cop opens it. You can just imagine *her* trying to arrest one of the Rogers scum. I can only feel contempt. Uncle Jack lifts his head and turns to look back, and that's when I see Aunty Margaret stood in the doorway. There she is, framed by the little house she and Uncle Jack have made lovely, have turned into a true home. There is Aunty Margaret crying and holding out a pathetic hand towards her husband while those Rogers bastards call her all the vile names that you can imagine. There is Aunty Margaret who has always been a friend and helper to everyone in this dreadful place. And there she is, standing all alone and crying, so that tears fall down my face too. Why are they taking Uncle Jack? What can have happened?

'We'd better get going.'

Andy has a hand on my arm. I turn to look at him, no longer caring whether or not he sees my tears. But Andy isn't paying any attention to me. I turn my face to look where he's looking and I see that the little shit Derek Rogers is staring across at us.

I just turn and start to walk. There's nothing I can do here. Andy is by my side.

'Rogers Bastards.'

I can't say anything, not even to agree. I can't get the images of Uncle Jack and Aunty Margaret out of my mind. I just can't. I think I'm realising for the first time that what I actually feel for Uncle Jack and Aunty Margaret is a kind of love. There, I've said it. It's like they're my own family. They're part of my childhood. Part of me, who I am. And it kills me that I can't do anything to help them. I'm managing to hold back the tears for now. But I know they'll just come flooding when I'm safe at home in my room. And of course I'm thinking of the Ruger. Who wouldn't be?

The Ruger P95 and the gun dog

It's early Saturday morning and I'm up, standing at my garden gate. It's that time of year when the mornings are cold and you know that there is mist in the air. All the cars parked at the roadside outside the houses are covered in beads of freezing dew. It's incredibly quiet.

I've been awake all night, unable to sleep. Clouded in a fog of sadness, I've been clicking the mouse and following pages on the internet.

RUGER P95

Weight: 765g

Overall Length: 184mm

Barrel Length: 99mm

I know this off by heart now. Not that I went out of my way to learn it; I wasn't even aware that I was reading it. My mind has been elsewhere; outside Uncle Jack and Aunty Margaret's house; down at the nick watching Uncle Jack being DNA swabbed and having his finger prints taken. That information will be on the records forever now, even if Uncle Jack isn't convicted of anything. Once they've got you recorded, they never let you go. Uncle Jack will be immortalised, along with the rapists and paedophiles and ponces and thugs.

RUGER P95

Grips: Black synthetic

Frame: Polymer

Sights: Fixed front and rear

I turn my head to look as the sound of a front door clicking open breaks the silence. It's the house next door and I nod a silent hello to our neighbour Alan, who spots me as he ushers his two excited Springer Spaniels out before him. The dogs stand on Alan's lawn looking back at him, their backsides wobbling as they wag their tails furiously. They're excited, yes, but they're patient. They're well brought up so they've learned to respect authority and not to fool around. Alan is wearing a green waxed Barbour jacket that looks heavy and is covered with voluminous patch pockets. He's wearing camouflage pants and hiking boots. Alan's front door clicks as he closes it softly behind him so as not to wake his still sleeping wife and not disturb the neighbourhood. I guess we're lucky to have a neighbour like Alan.

I watch the dogs fall in behind Alan as he strides along his garden path. They're still excited enough to pant, but they don't bark and they keep nice and close without him having to tell them.

'Starting to get cold.'

Alan smiles and rubs his hands together before reaching to open the gate.

'So long as it's not raining.'

My reply is feeble, but I have to say something if only to be polite. Actually, I'm staring at the long narrow green canvas bag slung over Alan's shoulder with a broad leather strap. I know that it contains a shotgun – Alan sometimes shares the spoils of his morning activities with us – but I have never seen it. Alan is careful to keep it concealed and unloaded until he's out in the woodland where he's going to shoot. He's lucky enough to be friendly with a farmer not too many miles away who has woodland. It's mostly wood pigeon that he kills, but there have been other game birds. Mum plucks and dresses them and we have game pie, which I'm told you would only normally see on the menus of fancy restaurants. Amazingly I like this game pie when we have it, even though now and then I've come close to breaking a tooth on lead shot.

'Rain, shine, it doesn't bother me.'

Alan is already opening the tailgate of his Subaru wagon, and the dogs are jumping in as he says this.

'Just getting out in the fresh air is good. And they love being out and about.'

He's nodding at the dogs as he slides the shotgun, still in its canvas carry-bag, into the back of the car.

I look at the dogs, just before the tailgate shuts to close them in. The spaniels are gun dogs. They've been bred to retrieve and trained to fetch shot game without eating or damaging it. Powerful jaws that can be very gentle.

Gun dogs. I find myself thinking about that as Alan slides into the driver's seat of the Subaru, closing the door carefully behind him, still respectful of the hour, of his neighbours. Surely it's wrong to call the dogs by that name. The dogs are only acting in accordance with their nature. Surely it's the people who carry the guns who are really the gun dogs.

RUGER P95

Calibre: 9mm

Capacity: 15 rounds

Rifling: 6 grooves, 1:10

Rifling of six grooves refers to the number of narrow slots cut in spirals along the inside of the barrel. 1:10 means that the rifling goes through one full rotation every ten inches – not that the Ruger has a ten inch barrel. Rifling keeps the bullet straight and accurate when it's fired.

Calibre 9mm means that the diameter of the inside of the barrel – and therefore the ammunition needed – is 9mm. That's a powerful round. And it carries fifteen such rounds in a fully-loaded magazine. The magazine is a metal box that slots into the base of the handle. I've heard the wannabe *Gangstas* at school talking about guns – as if they'd ever been near one – and saying that such and such a gun carries a twelve round clip or a ten round clip or whatever.

I now know for certain that they're talking crap. A clip is a disposable device that lets you speed-load a magazine.

The Ruger P95 in my hooded sweatshirt pocket carries a fifteen round magazine and it's fully loaded.

Alan's car pulls away from the kerb and I watch it as he accelerates gently down the road. The dogs are standing in the rear of the wagon, looking at me out of the window. I look back at them as I slide my hand into my pocket and my fingertips caress the polymer frame of the Ruger. Nah, they are not gun dogs. But maybe I am.

CHAPTER 8

Normal rules
no longer apply

It has started to drizzle with rain. Not enough to worry about, but enough for me to see the tiny droplets coating the fleece of my hooded sweatshirt. My hands are in the pockets and the fingertips of my right hand are absently caressing the cool polymer frame of the Ruger P95. I don't want to think about why the gun is in my pocket.

I'm standing on the pavement opposite Uncle Jack and Aunty Margaret's house. I'm still sad about what I saw last night. But I'm not weepy now. Actually, I'm numb. I want to know what exactly went on last night and why Uncle Jack has been arrested.

I'm looking over at the house, where the curtains are drawn because it's still pretty dark. It doesn't look as though anyone is up in the house because no electric light escapes the inevitable curtain gaps.

Every now and again, my gaze wanders to the side of the house and I have to look away quickly. I can't bear to look upon the battered little Nissan. It makes my fingers tighten on the cold object in my pocket. So I look at the house, and while I'm still feeling sad and angry and ashamed at my impotence last night, somehow looking at the house is more bearable.

I notice a twitch at the curtain. Someone in the house is awake. Whoever it is can't help but have seen me standing here. Not that I'm trying to hide. And it's not many seconds later that I see the front door slowly open. The hallway is dark behind, with no lights switched on. But there's a figure in the doorway, a woman dressed, and not speaking, not beckoning. Just looking at me looking at her. It's Aunty Margaret.

We stand like this, facing each other like melancholic gunslingers, for a few seconds that feel heavy and burdensome. But it's not a contest so I move first, crossing the road. As I approach, I see Aunty Margaret's face as I have never seen it before, so sad and disillusioned and defeated. A lump comes to my throat and I fight it down. I open the gate and step onto the concrete path leading to the front door. The lawn to the left of the path is billiard table-neat, the surrounding borders of dark soil all broken and even and weed-free, even though it's autumn and the best of the summer flowers have long since died.

As I approach the front door step, I look up at Aunty Margaret and her face just crumbles as the tears begin to flow.

'Oh Stevie...'

I put my arms around her and hold her to me. She is so dejected that she cannot even bring herself to hug me back and her arms hang limply down by her sides. We stand like this for a few moments with her sobbing against my shoulder, before I gently usher her back inside the house and I close the door on a prying world that just wouldn't care.

Minutes later, we're sitting in the living room with the curtains still closed, even though it's getting light outside. We're drinking tea and I'm eating slices of homemade sponge cake despite it being very early in the day. I know that I have to indulge Aunty Margaret right now.

'He only went outside to tell them to clear off. They were climbing all over the car and throwing bricks at the house.'

Bit by bit, through tears, I get the story. Uncle Jack went out to tell Rogers and his goblin followers to clear off after the rocks started to thump against the walls of their living room. And that's when it did get personal. Once Uncle Jack had dared remonstrate with them, rocks that had until that point accidentally hit the car and the house, now began to rain down on those twin targets with a purpose. Uncle Jack went out to remonstrate again and told these young children to clear off and make their mischief closer to their own homes.

'Who's going to make us?'

And you can just see the inbred Derek Rogers with his evil slitty eyes standing his ground against Uncle Jack, the Korean War veteran Grenadier Guardsman.

'I'll show you who.'

And Jack had gone out and grabbed the kid and smacked him on the back of his head, and had kicked his backside as the kid had turned to run away. Within half an hour, Derek Rogers was back and this time his brother Wayne was with him. They began shouting and swearing outside the house. And further damaging the car. Uncle Jack went out again to stop them. I can only imagine how distressing and terrifying it must have been for Aunty Margaret. Actually, I don't have to imagine; I can see it in her eyes right now.

Well the swearing and the vandalism and the intimidation continued until eventually, Uncle Jack called the police. And this is the part that bewildered Uncle Jack and Aunty Margaret but doesn't surprise me at all. It took half an hour to actually get to speak to someone, only to be told that no one could be despatched to come to the house. Friday night you see, and all units are busy in the town. You can hardly believe that can you? But let me tell you, you can never get a cop to come and deal with any kind of crime on our estate. They just don't want to know.

Five times Uncle Jack called those cops last night, only to be fobbed off each time like he was some kind of senile timewaster. Finally, much later, with Aunty Margaret crying fit to break your heart and a brave old soldier made a prisoner in his own home by yobbish filthy criminal scum, blue lights could be seen flashing outside the house. The police had turned up after all. Uncle Jack had gone out to greet them, to invite them in, ready to give a statement. But it hadn't been a statement that they'd been

after. They'd come to arrest Uncle Jack.
They hadn't come as a response to his
telephoned pleas for help. They'd actually
shown up as a response to a complaint by the
Rogers family. These filthy scum criminals
had called the police to complain that Jack
had assaulted their darling little boy, the
angelic Derek.

Oh come on, of course you can believe
it. The filth don't want to know about an
elderly couple being terrorised by the
violent, criminal Rogers family. But get the
chance to arrest and terrorise that elderly
couple themselves and they're out mob-
handed, quicker than you can spit. A quick
and easy arrest of an unresisting old man
and it helps their clear-up rate. They have
crime clear-up targets to meet and an arrest
and conviction of Uncle Jack will count for
just as much as solving a child-murder
or a rape. Oh yeah, they're brave and
trustworthy alright, the filth. I've known
stuff like this all my life, but for people like
Uncle Jack and Aunty Margaret, and even
people like my mum and dad, it all comes
as a shock. They still live in a past where

the police could be relied upon to see that order was maintained on the streets. And worked to uphold the law in favour of the gentle and the good against the violent and the criminal and the selfish.

I find out that Uncle Jack has been kept in the police station overnight and that Aunty Margaret is out of her mind with worry. I try to comfort her as best I can. In the end, I agree to go down to the police station with her. I don't know what we'll be able to do there, but it's the only thing Aunty Margaret wants. And I'm not about to let her go there alone.

CHAPTER 9
Gun dog dreaming

It's gone midnight. I'm out on the streets of our estate and there's no one about. I'm wearing dark jeans and a black cotton zip-up jacket and trainers. It's a dark night – lots of cloud and no moon. My hands are thrust deep into the pockets of my jacket. In the palm of my right hand I can feel the cool shape of the Ruger P95 that I carry with me. My fingers are curled gently around the black handgrip; my index finger lies along the trigger guard. I don't want any accidents; not like that stupid firearms cop who shot himself in the leg getting into his car. Christ, you couldn't make it up, could you? If it had been in a movie, you'd have fallen about laughing. Sometimes I feel that criminals with guns are less of a danger to the public than police with guns. The police, after all, have been known to shoot an innocent man in the head seven times at point blank range. Whatever the circumstances, that sounds more like frenzy than a controlled use of firearms. Make your own mind up on that one.

So I'm careful how I carry the Ruger and keep my fingers well away from the trigger. The Ruger does not have a manual safety catch. It fires with a double action of the trigger – first pressure cocks the weapon, second pressure fires it. After that, you just have to keep squeezing the trigger until the magazine is empty. Of course, there is a decocking lever that can be used to make it safe if you cock it and then decide not to shoot, or if you've finished shooting and there are still rounds in the magazine.

Anyway, I'm outside the Rogers' house. No point in wasting time, I walk straight into the yard and down the overgrown path to the front door. The Ruger is in my right hand now and my index finger is putting a light pressure on the trigger. I bang on the door with my left hand. I'm banging hard and long like I mean business. From inside the house there is swearing and shouting and I hear thumping footsteps clumping down the stairs. I step back as the door is thrown open and it is the hideously slobbish father of the clan. I don't give him time to swear at me as I raise the Ruger right in front of his face and squeeze the trigger twice. Two red holes appear in his face, one in the centre of his forehead and one in his cheek and he drops to...

'Stevie? Stevie!'

I've been daydreaming and Aunty Margaret is tugging at my sleeve to get my attention. We're sitting in the waiting area in the police station. We've been here for three hours now, waiting for them to let Uncle Jack go. In that time, I've been letting all kinds of scenarios run through my mind, all of them involving me roaming the streets with the Ruger and all of them involving me playing the tough man with the gun in my hand or just blowing away those who I consider to be expendable. Of course the Rogers clan have featured large in this latter category.

Now I look up as Aunty Margaret wants me to, and I can see Uncle Jack coming out of a doorway, head bowed, wearing the clothes that he'd been wearing when I'd seen him being arrested last night.

I get up, along with Aunty Margaret, and my hand slides inside my pocket. Of course, the Ruger isn't there – I'm not stupid enough to carry it to a police station. I'd made an excuse to call in at home on the way here and put it back beneath my bed. I'm checking involuntarily, probably because my daydreams have been so vivid.

A policewoman asks if we'd like her to organise a car to take us back home. Aunty Margaret and Uncle Jack are too wrapped up in relief, in each other, so I tell this policewoman, who is actually very pretty and is genuinely being kind, that we'll get a taxi. I have enough money in my pocket to pay for this, and the policewoman gives me a card with the number of a local taxi company and offers to let me use the telephone behind the counter. I find myself surprised at her genuine concern and compassion. Maybe the police aren't all bad after all. But then I only have to look at Uncle Jack and think about what we are doing here in the first place for that thought to evaporate. All the same, I can't lose the idea that individual police officers just *might* be human after all. A few of them.

So we take a taxi back to Uncle Jack and Aunty Margaret's house. Not because of some childish disdain for police hospitality, but because I just know that a police car turning up at the house will cause a frenzy of curtain twitching from the neighbours. And Uncle Jack and Aunty Margaret don't need to be subjected to that kind of embarrassing scrutiny.

In the house, over a cup of tea and more cake, I learn that they've charged Uncle Jack with assault. Like I predicted, they've taken his fingerprints and a DNA sample. So now the largest DNA database in the world has the records of a pensioner added to it. I stay with Uncle Jack and Aunty Margaret for a while and we try to be positive about things. But there isn't much to be positive about. What has happened is becoming only too familiar. If a householder defends his property against vandals and thieves, there's a good chance that the householder will be arrested and charged. My dad gets enraged when these cases make the news, but the problem is they make the news less and less. Not because they happen less and less. Quite the opposite; because they have become commonplace.

When I finally leave Uncle Jack and Aunty Margaret's house, Uncle Jack is crying. I walk slowly down their garden path, consciously avoiding looking to my right. I don't want to see the little car all smashed and dented. I can't bear it. As I walk down the road, towards my own house, a road now busy with cars, with people going about their Saturday business, I see my brother Sean and a couple of his friends.

'Where you been?'

Sean gets straight to the point.

'I've been around at Uncle Jack and Aunty Margaret's place.'

'You seen what happened to their car?'

'Yeah, I've seen.'

Sean shakes his head and looks away.

'It was them Rogers what done it, init.'

This is one of Sean's friends, Jason Lewis. Jason doesn't come from our estate. Actually, he lives a few miles away in a house on a leafy suburb. Jason's dad is a doctor and Jason's been friends with Sean since they started to play for a Sunday league football team together a few years back. Normally I'd laugh and take the piss out of safe suburban Jason talking in this manner. But today it just doesn't seem important.

'Yeah, it was.'

I can't bring myself to discuss it further.

'Somebody should take them out. It would be tons better around here without them.'

I shake my head. Sean is saying what Andy had said last night. It's right what they say – but only partly right. It would be better, yeah. But not tons better. The Rogers family are the worst and most obnoxious scum around here, sure, but there are others who would fill the vacuum if they went.

I realise that sometimes I make it seem like everyone living on our estate is lawless and selfish and criminal. You know, that's actually not the case. Most people are decent and hard working. But our estate's reputation is not built around the hard working and the law abiding. Its reputation comes from the minority of lawless clans that rule the streets. And they can do that because the police no longer care, and they know it. Nobody cares about what happens on estates like ours. And that's all I can think about, all the way home.

CHAPTER 10
Feeling like Travis Bickle

'Christ, that's ridiculous! Somebody should just shoot the bastards. They're like wild dogs.'

Listening to Dad venting his spleen like this makes me think of the Ruger. I can only agree, and I'd love someone to go around to the Rogers' place and blow the stinking lot of them away. But it isn't going to be me. There's a world of difference between daydreams and reality.

But something else has been intruding on my thoughts. *This will make you something. This is what counts around here.* It's what Big Roddy had said the night he gave me the Ruger to keep. At the time I'd thought he'd been watching too many films and listening to too much Public Enemy. But I know how it felt this morning, when I was out and about early on with the Ruger in my pocket. I definitely felt different this morning. And when I picture myself, in my mind I see me walking around with my hands in my pockets and not a worry in the world. A bit like the poster for that old movie with Robert De Niro. What's it called? *Taxi Driver*, yeah. I feel like Travis Bickle, before he really loses it. That's scary on so many levels. But most importantly, because maybe Roddy was right.

'Why wouldn't the police come out when Jack called them?'

Dad's still ranting and fuming about what's happened, like he never reads the papers or watches the news. I just let him get on with it. Then Dad reaches into his pocket and takes out a ten pound note and hands it to me.

'What's that for?'

'The taxi this morning. I'm really proud of you, looking after Jack and Margaret like that.'

Dad isn't looking at me when he says this. And I'm glad, because I'd be embarrassed too. We don't go in for that sort of soppy sentimental praise in our family. But I'm also wondering how proud Dad would be if he knew that I'd seen the Rogers kid and his goblin friends starting it all off last night and did nothing. I wonder how proud he'd be if he found out I'd stood and watched Uncle Jack getting arrested last night, then just walked on by. Just being reminded of that makes me ashamed all over again.

Mum looks up, 'I'm going to go around later, make sure they're alright. I'll take one of these cakes.'

She's been baking all afternoon. Probably to take her mind off it all.

'I'll come with you.'

That's Mum and Dad all over. They usually go down to the social club on Saturday nights. A few drinks, a few games of bingo. A few laughs with friends. But they'll forgo this to sit with Uncle Jack and Aunty Margaret. And, actually, there are a lot of people like Mum and Dad on this estate, so that you wonder why it's actually got such a bad reputation.

Mum looks at me and I see that she's weary with sadness.

'I called Catherine earlier.'

'I'm amazed she was in.'

I say this because I call Catherine all the time. Not because we're so wonderfully close or anything, but because I want her to keep telling me about university, about Brighton. I use her to stoke the fire that keeps my dream alight.

'She's coming back tonight. She's going to take a few days off.'

This is so unlike Catherine. She hardly ever comes back here. She has a job in Brighton and she uses that as the excuse, but when I talk to her I know that she just isn't comfortable back here. I don't mean with us, with Mum and Dad and me and Sean. I mean it's this town, this estate. She's moved on and she's no longer a part of it. And, amazingly, it's no longer a part of her either. That's the magic I so desperately want for myself. It's why I call her all the time, like somehow she'll one day give up a great secret that she's so far been keeping from me.

'Did she say what time she's getting here?'

'She'll be late. She's going to start out after she's finished work.'

And that means she *will* be late. It's a six-hour drive up from Brighton. But it's good because it means that I'll be in when she gets here. I'm going over to Andy's, but we're only going to hang out. Nothing special. And that reminds me; I'd better get going or I'm going to be late.

I'm walking down the road wearing a black cotton jacket and my hands are in the pockets. In the right pocket sits the Ruger, caressed by my fingertips. Usually I'm not as relaxed as this when I'm out and about. And what's really strange is that I didn't realise that until now. It's taken the degree of confidence and lack of fear that I'm now experiencing to make me understand just how tight and wary I usually am when I'm walking the streets. Surely there can only be one reason for that, and it's sitting in my pocket. That's not a comfortable thought at all. Because I'm analysing it now as I make my way over to Andy's in the fading light. And the only way that the Ruger can make me safe is if I am prepared to use it. I don't believe that I am. But I still feel that confidence it brings all the same. I have to fight the urge to take the Ruger out of my pocket and just look at it right there in the open.

After school activities

Another dreary Wednesday at school. The days are all starting to drag with the mornings getting darker and the evenings coming in quicker.

On the weekend, Catherine came and Catherine went. She spent all of Sunday with Uncle Jack and Aunty Margaret. I went round there with her for the morning, but I had to go home in the afternoon. I had a ton of homework to do. And on Sunday night, Catherine set off back to Brighton, so we didn't get to talk much at all. She's coming back this weekend though, driving up on Friday night. I think it shocked her to see how unhappy we all are, Mum and

Dad and Sean and me. And how depressed Uncle Jack and Aunty Margaret are. Before we even knocked on the door of Uncle Jack and Aunty Margaret's place, she saw the little Nissan all damaged and smashed up and she just broke down and cried. I had to hold her and comfort her for ages. Anyway, she's coming back at the weekend. It's taken something like this to remind her that we are her family and that some part of her will always be lodged here with us.

It's been a pretty dismal day at school today, all told, and I'm glad it's over now. I'm walking with Andy towards the school gates and we're in the middle of a crowd of kids who move faster now that it's home time than they ever did to get here in the morning. Andy and me are not going straight home tonight, despite the mound of homework we both have. We're going into the town centre to the shopping mall. Andy still has birthday money left over and he wants to get a couple of DVDs. He says he doesn't know what he wants to get but I'm betting he walks away with the first two Jason Bourne movies. I kind of hope he does, because I'd like to watch them again too.

'Stevie, Andy, wait!'

I turn to look and Rebecca Wardle is waving over at us. Rebecca is in the same class as me for French and, I have to admit, I like her. She's got this sort of dark blonde hair that's thick and kind of straight and her mum is a hairdresser so it always looks fantastic. Right now it's cut to look like Jennifer Aniston's and it suits Rebecca down to the ground. Our school is pretty casual about what we have to wear, but Rebecca is wearing this grey pleated skirt and a white blouse under a black sweater and these flat black leather shoes and white socks. She's sixteen like Andy and me and she looks pretty fantastic – she must be one of only a few girls at school who just look impossibly cute in a school uniform.

Andy and me stop and wait as she hurries over to us without running, carrying a pile of loose books awkwardly in her arms.

'Qu'est-ce que vous allez?'

She's all smiles and a little breathless as she asks. Andy just rolls his eyes, but I'm looking at the brilliant white smile and I can't help but think it's cute the way she talks in French like this.

'We're just going into town to get some DVDs.'

I answer in English for two reasons; my French is nowhere near as good as Rebecca's, and Andy doesn't take French.

Some of the books she's holding start to slip, and she reacts quickly to clutch them to her.

'Here, let me take those.'

'No, it's OK, I can manage.'

But she's already handing them to me, and we're starting to saunter slowly towards the school gates, the three of us.

'I was wondering if you wanted to come round tonight to do that French assignment. But if you're going to be out...'

Rebecca lives on our estate and sometimes we have got together to do French homework. I really should ask her out sometime. I want to. But I'm kind of scared that she'll say no. And I don't take rejection well at all. I mean, I think she likes me. And it's been her asking me to come around to do homework. But I keep wondering if that's all there is to it. Maybe one day I'll pick up the nerve to ask her.

'We're not going to be long.'

The words slip out and I look at Andy, who just shrugs to say he doesn't care either way.

'I could come around later if that's OK? What time do you want me to come?'

'I dunno... is seven o'clock OK?'

'Yeah, we'll be back ages before then.'

I nearly ask her if she wants to come into town with us right now, but I bottle out of it.

As we approach the gates, I notice the groups of kids milling about there. Lots are smoking already with absolutely no fear of reproach; seeing them makes me want to reach for my own smokes, but my hands are full with Rebecca's books.

Sammy Williams is standing among one group of lads. Sammy hasn't been to school all week, but he's here now. He's keeping pretty low key, I can tell, and so are those around him and it all seems so unnatural. Everywhere else the kids are noisy and boisterous. As you'd expect.

I can see what's happening of course; they're being as discreet as possible, but I can see the little packets being passed, palm to palm. It's like Sammy is giving out secret sweets. Only, let's face it, it's not sweets. It's some drug or other. I can't say which from here.

I watch Sammy break away from the group and walk quickly, his hands in his pockets and the peak of his Burberry cap pulled way down, to the corner of the road a little way away, where a couple of older lads, maybe eighteen or nineteen, are standing around, their eyes roaming everywhere. I don't recognise them so they are not from our estate.

We've already crossed the road as we approach Sammy and these other two. I see one of the older lads reach quickly into a pocket and just as quickly his hand comes out again and something is handed to Sammy, who stuffs it out of sight in a pocket of his own. It all happens so quickly and smoothly that you'd think they were stage conjurers.

Sammy turns to head back towards the school gates and, as he does, he notices us. Well, I think it's me he's noticing. It's pretty obvious that Sammy is a cog in the local drugs machine. And that the two older lads are bigger cogs in that same machine. I immediately think of Big Roddy and what he might have been doing over at the Concrete

Canyon where he was stabbed to death. Has Sammy simply taken Big Roddy's place?

Sammy nods at me and just carries on hurrying back to the school gates. What the hell did that nod mean? I'm thinking about the Ruger of course. Is Sammy going to ask for it back? In a way, it would be great to just hand it over to Sammy. At least then there would be no link between him and me. For now, I can't help feeling that the Ruger is somehow binding us, simply because Sammy knows that I'm holding it. On the other hand, I don't want to let it go.

'OK, I'll see you at seven then?'

Startled, I turn to Rebecca. We're standing next to a parked car at the bus stop and I know that it's her mum's.

'Wake up dream boy, pay attention.'

I grin sarcastically at Andy to let him know what I think of his comment as I pass the pile of books to Rebecca who has already got into the car.

'Yeah, seven. I won't be late.'

I shut the car door for Rebecca, nodding hello at her mum, who smiles back at me. Rebecca has already turned her attention to something else and I see her saying something to her mum as the car pulls away into the traffic. Now Andy and me are left standing at the bus stop, waiting for the bus to take us into town.

I keep thinking that those older boys on the street corner opposite are looking at me. As though they know that I have Roddy Thompson's gun. A shiver runs through me at the thought that it might have been *their* gun, loaned to Roddy.

I'm willing the bus to arrive, even though I know I'm probably just being paranoid. And anyway, it's not like being on the bus makes you safe. There was a story in the news recently where two kids were being obnoxious and actually smoking dope or something – I think it might even have been crack – on a bus somewhere. They wouldn't get off when the driver asked them, so that driver took his bus directly to the nearest police station. No kidding, that's what he did. And here's the great part. When he got out and went into the police station to report what was happening on his bus, parked right outside, you know what they told him? They told him that they couldn't come out to deal with it and suggested that he should call 999. Can you believe it? You'd better believe it because it truly happened. He's there, inside a police station, reporting a crime going on right outside the door, and they told him to call the emergency number.

So I don't know why I think I'll be safe when the bus comes. If those guys want to follow me onto that bus, I'll just be trapped. Not for the first time since I got it, I'm wishing that I had my gun with me.

CHAPTER 12

Is that a gun in your pocket or are you just pleased to see me?

So it's just gone ten o'clock at night and I'm out walking the streets again. I've been to Rebecca's place and we did the French homework. But I don't know how. We went up to her room to work while her mum stayed downstairs, setting the hair of one of their neighbours. Rebecca's mum often does work at home like that for extra money. Rebecca's dad left them years ago and there's only the two of them. They seem to get by OK. Rebecca always has cool things and cool clothes, and her and her mum go on holiday to Spain every year. So don't let me make you think they're in the depth of grinding poverty. It's not like a scene from Orwell's *Road to Wigan Pier* or anything.

Anyway, we go up to Rebecca's room and she shuts the door behind us. I put my books on the desk she has there under the window and when I turn round, she's standing right there in front of me.

'Do you like me?'

Well, what am I supposed to say to that?

'Yeah, of course I like you.'

I try to say it like it's the most obvious thing in the world and shouldn't really need saying. It's lame but it's a start.

'No, I mean *really* like me...'

She's wearing this cute little fitted top and Kate Moss-style kind of cinched in waistcoat over these neat little shorts and she has the straightest whitest teeth and... well, next thing you know, she's raising herself up on her toes and her eyes are starting to close as her face comes close to mine and her lips part slightly so that I can taste her minty breath. It's something else, kissing Rebecca, let me tell you. But I'm not giving it my full attention, oh no. Because all I can think of as she's slipping her arms around me and slipping her sweet wet tongue between my lips, is that she mustn't feel the Ruger lying heavy in my jacket pocket. And I almost blow it by nearly pissing myself laughing at an old joke that springs to mind – *is that a gun in your pocket or are you just pleased to see me?* When we come up for air eventually, I begin to slip the jacket off.

'See. That wasn't so bad, was it?'

I'm glad she's talking, looking at me, because I'm sure she'll see the way my jacket hangs heavy at the pocket with the Ruger in it and she'll ask me what it is.

'Not bad at all.'

I'm smiling and maintaining eye contact with her as I put my jacket over the back of a chair. Once it's safely out of touching range, I take her in my arms again, and this time... well, it's just out of this world.

We did actually finish the French assignment, believe it or not, but we did spend a lot of time kissing and holding each other and talking crap too. When it came time to leave, and we came downstairs, I swear that Rebecca's mum was looking at us with a twinkle in her eye. Like she knew we hadn't just been working up there. In fact I'm sure she knew. She's cool, is Rebecca's mum. But I think I must have felt a little embarrassed all the same, because I've gone and left my homework and stuff at Rebecca's house. I'm trusting that she'll bring it to school with her on Friday when we next have French. And it's funny, because we've not said anything, but I'm pretty sure that me and Rebecca are now going out together. That's how it feels to me anyway. I hope that we are.

So now I'm out walking in the dark, beneath the orange glow of the street-lamps, and I'm thinking about all this, and what those kisses meant, and how there's a lot more than kissing that I'd like to be doing with Rebecca. Anyway, I'm thinking about all this, and it's actually cool to be out walking and going over and over stuff in my mind, so I'm not going straight home. I'm already on the far side of our estate on streets that I don't know well, but I'm far from being lost. It's getting cold, like there's going to be a frost in the night, and I slip my hands into the pockets of my black cotton jacket. And my right hand comes instantly into contact with the cold black angular polymer frame of the Ruger.

RUGER P95

Double Action Trigger Pressure: Fourteen Pounds

Single Action Trigger Pressure: Five Pounds

Firing Pin Action Point: Centre Fire

It gets me to thinking about earlier. I'm in my room at home and it's after I got back from town with Andy – he did get the two Jason Bourne movies – and before going over to Rebecca's. I have the Ruger on my desk and I'm prowling the internet in search of more information about it. There's lots. But one site even shows me how to strip it down.

First I clear the pistol of ammunition, in other words, I make sure that there isn't a round already in the firing chamber. Then the slide, the mechanism that ejects the spent cartridge and loads the next round from the magazine, is locked to the rear with the slide lock. I put my finger in the ejection port where spent cartridges are spat out, and I press the ejector down. Now I can let the slide run off the frame by releasing the slide lock. The slide lock is then pulled away from the frame. I pull the guide rod and spring away from the barrel, and then remove the barrel from the slide. See; easy when you know how. I must have practised stripping it down and putting it back together about twenty times. I still can't do it blindfold, but I have to say, I'm getting pretty good.

It's not totally late so the streets aren't empty. There's the odd car about here and there, and people I recognise but don't really know, going about their business. Again, there's flickering light from televisions and it's just an ordinary average night on our estate.

In the distance I hear high revving
engines and screeching tyres. That can
only be joyriders – kids in a stolen car.
I'm listening out and there it is, the police
siren. So they're in hot pursuit through the
crowded narrow streets of our estate. The
screeching tyres and high revving engines
are getting closer. I'm watching out in the
direction they're coming from. And now
here they are. That was quick, and I can
see the hot hatchback coming careering
towards me, lurching between the parked
cars to either side, hitting some of them as
the driver fights for control. And there, not
far behind, is the police car, complete with
blue flashing lights and wailing sirens.
Without even realising it, I'm standing as
far back on the pavement as I can. It's not
like these high-speed chases haven't ended
with innocent people maimed or killed in
the past. Actually, that's happened often
enough to be frightening. I smile at the
irony; that the only time we seem to see a
police presence on our estate is when they
are in hot pursuit like this and run the risk
of endangering life and property every bit as
much as the yobs they're chasing. But even

I acknowledge that it must be a tough call for the police; they're damned if they don't go after kids in a stolen car, and damned if they do and there's an accident. Just a pity they don't put as much effort into making these streets safe for the likes of Uncle Jack and Aunty Margaret.

The screeching tyres and the revving engines and wailing sirens are already a distant echo as I continue my aimless wander. I'm already on the edge of the estate where it gives way to a couple of country roads that will eventually take you up to the high moorlands. There's an embankment with some steps leading down into an underpass that takes you under the brightly lit dual carriageway cutting its curving way past the town centre and linking up with the motorway. I'm amazed at how busy the dual carriageway is. Where are all these people going? On the far side, the underpass brings you out onto a darkened industrial estate. From there, even darker roads will eventually lead you onto ever brighter and busier roads until eventually you'll be in the town centre.

I'm already in the underpass and heading for the far side with the muted trucks and cars rumbling overhead when I realise that I would never usually walk down here at night. But I'm not the least bit tense. My hands are in the pockets of my jacket and my right hand is loosely holding my Ruger. What could possibly happen to me?

I'm sauntering through the deserted access roads of the industrial estate, and I'm vaguely heading towards the town centre when I come to the canal bridge. I look down at the inky black water, still as glass, and the unlit towpath that runs alongside. The canal runs right through the heart of the city, between the derelict and deserted and run-down factory buildings with their crumbling brick walls and dirty cracked and broken windows. The only light down there on that towpath comes when the canal goes under a bridge and the light from the street-lamps lining the road above spill down and spread for a few metres to either side.

Even here I feel cool and loose. Yeah, that's right; I'm walking along the canal towpath. You hear stories about junkies and vagrants and God knows what congregating under the darkened bridges of the canal, but I can't say I feel wary of anything. Why should I? I'm walking with my hands in my pockets just like Travis Bickle from *Taxi Driver* and I have 9mm centre-fire double action semi-automatic protection in my pocket. The only thing that nags at the back of my mind to worry me a little bit is the thought that perhaps a part of me *wants* something to happen. I slide that thought quickly out of reach.

It's funny down here by the canal. You can hear cars and stuff, but they don't seem real, like you're listening to a background soundtrack that's totally unrelated to where you are. I stop and arch my head back to look up at the sky. Beyond the black silhouettes of the crumbling factories, the sky is glowing orange from the lights in the town centre. None of it seems real at all. And I'm so alone down here that I feel like I'm in my own little kingdom.

I don't know for sure how long I spend down there, but it's gone midnight before I'm back on the familiar streets of the estate. Mum and Dad won't be worrying. I've been out late before with Andy. Mum will probably be awake though until I get in. She tells me that she doesn't sleep until I'm home and I believe her. I suppose it's selfish of me to have stayed out so late knowing that, but I haven't done it on purpose. It just didn't cross my mind – which is exactly what selfish means. I'm not going to beat myself up about it though.

The way I'm coming back onto the estate, there's this row of shops that I have to pass. They're set back from the road, and a couple of them are boarded up, but there's a kebab shop there that will be closed now, and a little mini supermarket which we call *the vacuum shop* because it carries hardly any stock. Anyway, as I approach, I see a group of four kids in hooded sweatshirts and baggy combat pants lounging about in front of these shops. I can't recognise them from here, and normally I'd be wary of them, but I'm not tonight. You know why.

So I'm walking towards them casually and they start to move so that they are going to be blocking my path. At this point, I'm amazingly calm. I wouldn't normally be, I know, but I am now. So calm that I'm even *noticing* that I'm calm.

'Where you been man?'

I'm stopped in front of this group now and I recognise the kid that's talking. He's from my school but a couple of years below me. He'd be in Sean's year.

'Nowhere. Just out walking.'

I'm still calm and my hands are in my pockets. Two of the kids are smoking spliffs and grinning. The kid who had spoken reaches inside his sweatshirt and my hand tightens around the grip of my Ruger. And I'm *still* calm.

'So, what you got?'

I could have guessed that this was going to happen. The kid has a knife and it's not far from my throat and could even slash my face easily enough.

'I've got money, and a phone.'

You know, I nearly blow it by laughing out loud. I think I want to laugh at my rotten acting, trying to sound intimidated and compliant. Because I sure as hell don't feel that way at all. I'm making a big deal about getting something out of my jacket pocket. I seem to be struggling, but it's part of my act.

Suddenly my hand is free and I've taken a quick step back at the same time as I thrust out my right arm. I've knocked the hand holding the knife away from me and I'm looking down the gunsights along the top of the Ruger, and right into the kid's eyes. I can weigh it all up like I'm some kind of psychologist. He's angry and he's confused and he's wondering if the gun is real. And all this in a second.

'Drop it.'

The words are mine. And they are not angry and they are not excited. But I hear in my own voice an authority that I've never heard before.

'Fuck, he got a rod.'

'That a wicked iron, man.'

Two of the other kids but I'm ignoring them.

'Drop it or I blow your head clean off.'

I can't understand why my voice is so calm, why I'm not swearing and screaming. But something about my calm voice is getting through to the kid in front of me. I see his eyes flicker for a moment while he's weighing up this situation, but soon enough the knife clatters to the ground.

I take a step forward and jam the gun barrel hard into this kid's face so that he staggers back. I hear the sound of footsteps running away. His friends have deserted him.

'On your knees.'

The kid is trembling, but he remains standing.

'Don't shoot me.'

I ram the gun into his mouth so that for a moment I wonder if I've broken his teeth.

'On your knees.'

This time, he goes to the ground, the barrel of the Ruger still hard against his gums. I look down and see the blood around his lips like a clown's make-up. And with a ridiculous flash of awareness, I realise I'm just emulating what I've seen on TV and in movies. I don't really know what I'm doing or what I should do next.

'OK, so what *you* got?'

I'm mimicking his voice to humiliate him. Amazingly, when he reaches into his pocket, he pulls out a roll of notes. And yes, of course I take the money from him. It's not theft when you steal from a thief, is it?

It's only when I'm nearly home that I start to tremble. I feel excited and exhilarated. That's the adrenaline still coursing through me. I wasn't quite Travis Bickle back there, and I didn't even fire a shot. But I'm pretty sure I know how Travis Bickle felt.

CHAPTER 13
Scratching the itch

I haven't slept. I'm not tired though, and I know what's kept me awake. I've been lying there in bed all night, holding the Ruger in my hand. I've run through so many scenarios, with me and my gun at the centre of the action, that I reckon I could write a good movie script. But there's one thing more than ever that I'm aching to do. I want to pull the trigger. I want to see what it feels like. I want to know what sound it makes and if it kicks. Several times in the night I found my index finger just starting to squeeze at the trigger. Of course I was always able to stop myself; I haven't gone crazy.

So I've wagged off school today. You won't believe this, but I feel a little bit guilty about that. Still, I'll easily pick up on what I've missed, and it's only going to be this one day. I've come out here to the woodland a few miles outside of town. It's quite a big area of pine trees with lots of pathways where people walk their dogs and even ride horses. At the weekends, especially in the summer, there are lots of people around. But now, in the autumn on a Thursday, it's empty. At least I've not seen anyone. There's just the sound of dogs barking way off in the distance to suggest that there might be someone out here, giving the animals some exercise and a welcome break from the backyard. But, like I say, I've seen no one.

I've been traipsing between the trees, far from the pathways, for over an hour. I want to get to somewhere lonely. You know full well why I'm here. I'm going to fire the Ruger. I have an urge to feel it come alive in my hand. It's almost like I think that the very act of squeezing the trigger will do just that; breathe some life into it. And do you notice how I talk about *squeezing* the trigger? That's something I've read about; when you fire a gun, you apply progressive pressure to the trigger, you don't just jerk at it. If you want to be accurate, that is. When you first fire the Ruger, it takes fourteen pounds of pressure on the trigger to cock the hammer. And five pounds of pressure to fire it. That's what I've read. I have absolutely no idea what fourteen pounds of pressure feels like. Or five pounds. That's what I'm here to find out though. It's an itch that I absolutely have to scratch.

I come out of the tree line and into a pretty large clearing. The ground is rust-coloured with fallen pine needles and somewhat springy because of them too. It's almost silent here, and with the trees all around and a low grey sky above, it's like being in a box, like you're somehow removed from the world at large. If I listen carefully, I can hear a backdrop of constant car noise, but it's so way off in the distance that it doesn't really intrude on the quiet in this place.

Like I said, this clearing is pretty big, and there's a sort of small lake in it, about a hundred metres or so across. It's actually quite spooky, because a kid died in this lake last year. Well actually, when I say died, I should say he was killed. It was in the holidays last summer. Loads of kids come into these woods to play, and one day, some kids were here, and there was some kind of argument about a stolen bike or something, and one kid was thrown into the lake. And when this kid tried to climb out, the other kids threw rocks at him and stuff and stopped him. And, eventually, he went under the water and drowned. We're talking about kids who are about twelve years old here. I don't know them, because they're not from my estate and they don't go to my school, but I know that it's a true story because it was in the papers. But not on the front pages. It was nowhere near sensational enough for that.

So, like I said, it feels spooky here by this lake. And that's even despite the fact that I'm carrying the Ruger in my pocket. Let's face it, a gun is no use against a ghost. And you can stop sniggering; you wouldn't find it funny if you were out here alone, I'm telling you. This place does feel strange.

So I'm back in among the trees and I've walked well away from that lake. It might as well be here as anywhere. I take the Ruger out of my pocket and the synthetic black grip rests against the palm of my right hand while my fingers curl loosely around it. My index finger rests alongside the trigger guard and does not touch the trigger at all. I hold the gun out in front of me, my feet are planted shoulder width apart and my knees are slightly bent. The handle of the gun is resting against the palm of my outstretched left hand for stability, just like I've read in articles on the internet, and have seen in movies and on television. I'm looking straight along the top of the barrel. The polymer frame is glistening black. I'm aiming at the trunk of a tree about twenty feet away as I slip my finger inside the trigger guard. I begin to squeeze, slowly. Nothing's happening. I think I'm a bit tense waiting for the bang, not knowing what to expect. I continue to squeeze. Surely that's fourteen – BANG!

Actually, it doesn't bang, not in the way that a firework bangs, or guns in old movies bang. It's loud enough, sure, but it's a metallic sound that dominates, the sound of the slider knocked back to eject the spent cartridge and pick up the next round from the magazine, loading it into the chamber.

I look at the tree in front of me. I can see where the bullet has hit it, but it's way higher than I'd been aiming. The recoil from the gun was not as strong as I'd been expecting, but I hadn't been ready for when the shot was going to come. When it had, it had taken me by surprise, and I'd let the Ruger jump in my hand. I'll be more prepared next time.

I take aim again, but now it's already cocked; it's only going to take five pounds of pressure on the trigger to fire it this time. I hold it a little bit tighter, plant the base of the handle a little firmer in the palm of my left hand. I begin to squeeze the trigger. BANG! That's better. Much lower, but it's pulled to the left a little. One more shot, I'm thinking, just to get the measure of it, and I'll call it a day. Now don't go thinking that I'm packing in early because firing the gun is unnerving me or something. That's far from being true. It's actually given me a hard-on, if you want the actual truth. Big Roddy had said that having a gun is what made you something. Well last night, with that kid kneeling terrified at my feet and with the blood from his gums all over the end of the barrel of my Ruger, I'd started to realise just what Roddy had meant. But here, now, actually pulling the trigger, feeling and hearing the gunshot, it's the most exciting feeling imaginable. So no, don't go thinking I'm packing in because I'm soft; I'm going to call it a day because I only have fifteen rounds of ammunition. And how the hell would I go about getting any more? I just don't want to waste it. Actually, right now I only have thirteen rounds. And that will soon be twelve.

I'm aiming at where a patch of bark has been torn away by my last shot. Breathe out, hold, squeeze – BANG! Not bad, even if I do say so myself. Two inches right and about an inch above where I'd wanted it to go. The websites all talk about balance and how much play there is in the trigger when they're reviewing guns. I don't really know how to judge those things, but something must be right with this Ruger P95, because I am an absolute novice and I can already put a bullet pretty much where I want it to go. A lot of that must be down to the gun, not any skill on my part.

I look down to where the spent cartridge cases have been ejected. I pick them up, noticing the small indentation on the base of each of them where the firing pin has hit them. I put them in my jacket pocket along with the Ruger. All in all, I'm feeling rather pleased with myself.

You talkin' to me?

Coming out of the woods I'm feeling good. I've got my Ruger in my pocket of course, and my hands tucked in. I'm trying to walk like Travis Bickle from that old movie I mentioned earlier, *Taxi Driver*. I'm looking down but I'm relaxed and afraid of nothing.

From the woodland, there are two ways to get home. The long way takes you into the town centre and then down past the canal, onto the industrial park and under the dual carriageway. The quick way takes you through the concrete labyrinth of run-down flats where I was beaten up and robbed once upon a time. Where Big Roddy was stabbed and bled to death just a few short days ago. Normally, it would be a no-brainer; despite the fact that it would add an extra half hour to my journey time, I would always head for the town centre. Of course, you know where I'm headed today though. Another no-brainer, really.

I see it, the Concrete Canyon, long before I reach it; the grey concrete slabs from a distance looking like fallen monoliths at Stonehenge. But I feel no apprehension at all. I just carry on down the paths at the edges of the fields, making my way towards it. And before you know it, I'm there, stepping into it. There are patches of tended grass surrounding this high-rise monstrosity. The council plants trees every now and then, but they are slashed and stripped or uprooted within days. I can see the poor ruined saplings, no taller than me, but broken and bent where dimwits have split their slender trunks. And the areas of grass are covered with litter and debris, much of it from where dogs or urban foxes have ripped into refuse sacks left out near to the overflowing bins. It all adds to the oppressive atmosphere so that it's hard to believe that there are actually people living here in the midst of all this. It's something for me to consider whenever I lament the rough nature of my own estate.

I'm walking across a square of grey flagstones, a pedestrian area between two of the high-rises. Above me are walkways. To my right there is a row of boarded-up shops, covered in graffiti and protected behind strong rusty steel railings. Who the hell would want to run a business here? It seems unnaturally quiet and oppressive to me. Oppressive. That's the word that keeps coming to me. Oppressive.

There are few people about – just a couple of prematurely-aged girls standing next to a pram and a pushchair. These girls will be teenagers, but they look older and rougher and dirtier than girls should. They are fat and greasy and don't care, and you can see their tattoos. Do I have to mention that they are smoking? I can't help but think what dead end lives these girls must lead. Lives without hope. No dream of university in Brighton for them. All of a sudden I realise just how lucky I am.

On my right there is a large gap between two buildings. Beyond this gap is the entrance to a multi-storey car park. No sane person would ever park a car in there. All the levels are dark, even in daylight, and I can see rusty burned-out wrecks on the ground floor level. This is what happens to cars that the joy-riders from this estate steal.

'Oi, fuck off!'

The words echo in this empty Concrete Canyon. I look up, trying to see who is doing the shouting. On a walkway five floors up, I see a malevolent face peering down and focusing on me. The little bastard can't be more than ten years old. Already he is as territorial as a dog. One of the myriad feral scum that are whelped in this hell hole. The way that the grey concrete of the buildings seems to merge with the low grey clouds overhead makes this place feel more alien and oppressive than you can possibly imagine. Oppressive.

Over to my left, a fair way away, I can see three boys. One of them is Sammy Williams. The other two I also recognise. They'd been outside the school yesterday afternoon, just down the road from the school gates. They'd been the ones supplying Sammy with whatever God forsaken substances he'd been moving onto the kids who'd been keen to take the samples.

I don't know if I'm reckless or stupid or both, but I stop and stand watching them for a while. They don't notice me. One of the older boys turns quickly and the door of the flat behind him, covered in a sheet of rusty steel, opens smartly, just a little bit to allow him access, then just as quickly shuts behind him. Sammy and the other boy are just lounging about. I don't even know if they're talking. Then the steel covered door opens again and the boy who'd gone in comes out. Sammy hands something over so fast that it seems like sleight of hand. The boy hands over a plastic bag. Sammy examines it for a moment then slips it into the pocket of his grey polar-fleece jacket. I'm wondering if that's why Big Roddy was killed here. Was that what he was doing here in the first place? Was Big Roddy getting involved in the distribution of some chemical crap or other when it all went sour on him? Is Sammy Williams now picking up where Big Roddy left off? Is this why Big Roddy had got himself the Ruger in the first place? My Ruger.

I realise that I've been standing here just staring for longer than is wise, even with the Ruger in my pocket for protection. Fact is, in this place I'm guessing that there's a lot more firepower available than I'm carrying. And, more to the point, there are the kind of scum here that wouldn't hesitate to shoot, just on a whim. I'm cursing myself now for being stupid enough to come through here in the first place. The Ruger has given me a false sense of immortality. It comes as a shock to realise that I'm only too mortal after all.

Sammy still has his back to me. But one of those older boys is looking past Sammy. He seems to be looking in my direction. Is he looking at me? I'm sure that he is. Oh fuck, he is, he's looking at me. I'm scared, I'm like a rabbit in headlights on a country road and I'm frozen to the spot. The boy staring at me raises his arm very slowly and extends it in my direction. With his hand and fingers, he makes an imitation gun pointing right at me, and mimics firing a shot. Even from this distance I can tell that he's not smiling and that his eyes are blank and soulless. Sammy turns his head to see what this boy has been pointing at, and notices me. He just shakes his head, like he's saying how stupid I am just being here. I can't help but agree, and this breaks the spell. I turn and carry on walking, hurrying to the road beyond this horrible place with its horrible memories – which have all come flooding back.

Before I get to the road, I pass the place where Big Roddy bled to death. There's still a dark stain on the concrete from his blood, and a few bunches of already decayed and dirty flowers, but I don't stop to inspect any of it. I just want to get home.

The rest of the way home, I didn't feel like Travis Bickle at all. I stopped in at the video store and rented a copy of that movie, *Taxi Driver*, on DVD. I've watched it twice already, preferring that to going into school for the afternoon and having to make an excuse for the morning. I played it on my computer in my room.

It's tea time now, and I'm standing in front of my long dressing table mirror with my shirt off. My Ruger is held loose in my right hand. Very suddenly, I thrust out my arm and the Ruger is pointing at my image in the mirror. I'm nodding my head almost imperceptibly, mocking my reflection.

'I'm faster than you, you scum. I saw you coming.'

Yeah, I know how ridiculous this is; I'm acting out a scene from the movie, where Travis Bickle is standing in front of a mirror practising a quick-draw. Travis is wearing an army jacket and he has a spring-loaded mechanical device inside the sleeve that automatically delivers the gun into his hand quicker than you can see. I don't have any of this, but I can point the Ruger and say the words. It's all about attitude.

'I'm standing here. You make your move.'

The Ruger is pointing right into my face very suddenly. I'm fast. I really am. I drop my hand to my side. And now I'm looking right into my own eyes, and it's like my reflection really is a different person.

'You talkin' to me?'

Pause.

'You talkin' to me?'

I look around, theatrically.

'Then who the hell else are you talking to? You talkin' to me? Well, I'm the only one here. Who the fuck do you think *you're* talking to?'

I hear footsteps thumping up the stairs so I hastily hide the Ruger away. I know that it's my brother Sean, and it's no surprise that he just bursts into my room without knocking. I'm already sitting at the computer by then, pretending to read something on the screen.

'Hey bro! You weren't at school today.'

I ignore him.

'Couple of kids was talkin'. Sayin' you was out last night carryin' a wicked piece of tin. They say you turned a kid over.'

I'm still ignoring him.

'I said it couldn't be you. Unless you'd clobbered the kid with a book or something.'

I turn around at this and look him straight in the eye, pointing my fingers like they're an imitation gun.

'You talkin' to me?'

The centre of attention

Friday morning and I'm walking to school. To be honest, I'm happy to be going back to some kind of normality. Yesterday was pretty freaky. Especially that business in front of my mirror.

So it's good to be walking through the school gates with Andy, who I've just caught up with, and seeing the usual clowning yelling sullen faces around and about as we pass on through.

'So what happened to you yesterday?'

'I didn't feel well.'

Andy is looking at me like already he doesn't believe me. After all, I never usually miss a day.

'Look, I could have come in for the afternoon, but in the end I just couldn't be arsed, OK?'

Andy smiles and nods.

'I thought you'd sneaked off with Rebecca Wardle to be honest. Home alone for the day, and the chance of getting jiggy together...'

'So what makes you think we didn't?'

Andy looks at me like he's a lawyer from a TV show about to play his trump card.

'Because Rebecca was here yesterday with an armful of books, and looking for you.'

'Well, I was at home with the runs. Happy now?'

The books must have been the French stuff that I'd left at her place on Wednesday night. I hadn't expected her to bring them in until today because we didn't have French until today. Perhaps she brought them in as an excuse to see me. What? You never know. As if she needs an excuse after Wednesday night anyway. We're going to go out somewhere this weekend. We're going to decide what we're doing after French class.

'You should have texted me. I would have sent her round to wipe your arse.'

Andy likes toilet humour.

'You can be very funny at times. Pity this isn't one of them.'

It's crappy banter, but it's always good natured stuff between me and Andy.

I'm becoming aware of some of the kids stopping and giving me long hard looks as we walk past. Not all of them, not by a long shot. But some of the younger kids, definitely.

I'm remembering what Sean said, about the word going out. I don't think I like that at all, the idea of the word going out about me having a gun and using it to go out on the rob. It's not as if I'm like that old gangster, what was his name? John Dillinger. I'm wishing that I'd been more careful and less cocky and that I hadn't used the gun at all. I don't like being the centre of attention, and the last thing I want is to get a reputation as someone who carries a gun and likes to flash it about. That's a quick way to ending up dead. I suddenly feel cold and pale and genuinely sick.

'Hey, Stevie! Stevie, wait!'

Andy and me both turn and it's Rebecca and she's hurrying after us. We wait for her to catch up.

'Where were you yesterday? I was looking for you. I had your books.'

She's a little out of breath from hurrying to catch up with us as she hands my books to me. She's looking so cute that I've forgotten all about being the centre of attention.

'I wasn't feeling well so I stayed home.'

We're walking along together now, but slowly. Rebecca has linked her arm through mine, and I have to say, it makes me feel good.

'I thought you'd decided to avoid me.'

She's smiling when she says this, so I know she's not serious.

'You should have called. I had my mobile with me.'

'I don't even have your number yet.'

That's true. We haven't swapped numbers.

'You might have heard some interesting sounds if you *had* called.'

Trust Andy to lower the tone.

'Very funny.'

Rebecca looks puzzled.

'I had an upset stomach yesterday.'

I feel that I have to explain, but I give Andy a sharp look just the same. Actually, I'm thinking that Rebecca *might* have heard some interesting sounds indeed. Like the automatic reload mechanism of a Ruger P95 echoing through the woods.

And then the bell goes. We're walking through the herd of kids, all heading for the main doors. Just another school workday then. But at least it's Friday. I have plans to make with Rebecca. And Catherine is coming home tonight. Plenty of things to smile about.

At last the school day is over and there's a weekend to look forward to, and not much homework either. A cold mist has come down as I walk towards the school gates among the gangs of noisy kids. I'm looking out for Andy. And Rebecca, truth be told.

They've got to pass through the gates, so I'll wait for them there. Neither of them will have come out before me because I got out just before the bell today.

Leaning against one of the brick pillars that support the school gates, I see Sammy Williams. He's already seen me, and he's looking right at me. He's beckoning me over, so I have no choice. My hands are in my pockets and I'm trying to appear cool and unruffled as I approach him.

'Hey, Sammy...'

It's another, younger kid, but Sammy doesn't even look at him; just waves him away with a couple of sweeps of his hand. Before you know it, I'm standing there, right in front of him.

'Saw you over at the Concrete Canyon yesterday.'

I can't see Sammy's eyes – the peak of his Burberry cap is pulled way down – until he lifts his head slowly and he's fixing me with them. They're totally empty of any emotion.

'Yeah. I was just taking a short cut home.'

This is true; I was.

Sammy nods slowly, like he's pondering this.

'Heck of a place to be taking a short cut. A lot of bad people over there at the Canyon. You know what happened to Roddy.'

I look away because his eyes are unnerving.

'Yeah. It was even on the telly. To be honest, I think that's why I went that way. To see where it happened.'

I'm hoping that this sounds plausible. Sammy nods his head slowly again.

'Well the same thing could happen to you. You should bear that in mind.'

'I will. It was bloody scary just being there.'

There's absolutely no way whatsoever that Sammy Williams gives a shit whether I live or die, so there's more coming. And I have a good idea what this little talk is really about.

'There's been some talk going around.'

This is it; this is what I've been expecting.

'Word is that you were out the other night. Carrying a rod and threatening to smoke some kid while you were robbing him.'

I must look as pale and frightened as I feel because Sammy shakes his head and smiles, almost laughs.

'Don't worry. I've been telling people that it couldn't have been you, that there's been some mistake.'

I can feel my legs starting to shake. Sammy puts a hand on my shoulder.

'Thing is, we both know that it *could* have been you. That thing you were holding for Big Roddy, right? You *are* keeping it safe, right?'

That thing is my Ruger P95. Christ, this moron doesn't know the first thing about it, calling it a thing. I just nod though.

'Yeah. It's safe.'

Sammy nods again, slowly, like he's thinking something over.

'Well, you've done a good job. I owe you one. Time that you handed it back, though, I think.'

I almost blurt out that there's no way, but sanity prevails. Just.

'In the alleyway behind the shopping precinct tomorrow afternoon at about half past two. Bring it there. The thing is, Roddy had only ever borrowed it. And now the guys who own it are asking for it back. OK?'

I'm nodding agreement. What else can I do? I know the shopping precinct. Sammy is talking about the shops where the kids confronted me the other night.

'Like I say, I owe you one. I'll score you some good blow tomorrow if you like. I won't forget what you've done.'

And he goes and pats me on the cheek, like he's my dad or something, just as he turns to walk away. I feel sick right then, but I notice Andy and Rebecca standing over on the far side of the road, watching. I cross to join them.

'What were you doing with him?'

I can hear the disapproval in Rebecca's voice, and I can't blame her for it. The last thing she needs is a boyfriend mixed up with Sammy Williams and all of his trouble.

'It's nothing. He was just asking me if I'd seen Dwayne Riley. You know, that retard who hangs out with Sammy and that lot sometimes. I told him, I haven't seen him in ages. It's pushing it to think that freak will turn up at school.'

I think that that's a pretty good lie, and it seems to please Rebecca and Andy. We start walking towards home. I've snapped out of the shock of Sammy Williams wanting the Ruger back. I'm not even going to think about it.

'You fancy coming around tonight to watch a DVD or something? Mum's going out, so if you feel like it...'

Catherine's coming home tonight; but she won't be here until late. And of course I'd love to spend time with Rebecca. Who wouldn't? I look over at Andy; we usually get together on Friday nights. Rebecca sees me looking.

'You can come too, if you want...'

It sounds a half-hearted invitation and only a half wit wouldn't pick up on it.

'Really? That would be fantastic. Do you want me to bring anything?'

Rebecca is fighting to find the right thing to say but I know when Andy is joking and it's all he can do to stop himself laughing right now. I send him a look and now he *is* laughing.

'OK, OK! I wouldn't want to spend a night watching you two playing twister together anyway.'

Rebecca gives him a playful thump. I slip my hand into hers and she curls her fingers around mine as we walk. I'm almost not thinking about my Ruger at all.

The grass is greener

I wake up and I look at the clock sitting on my bedside table. It's ten o'clock, and that's very late for me. I can hear activity in the house below me. From Sean's room next door, I can hear the sound of Saturday morning television, muted only by the wall and not by any consideration on Sean's part.

The reason I've slept in is easy enough to work out; I was very late getting to sleep. I mean, I'd been to Rebecca's place until about ten, and you know, that was really cool. She's more amazing than even I had thought and she knows so much about films and stuff. I was telling her about *Taxi Driver* – obviously without mentioning that I had a gun and sometimes fancied myself as Travis Bickle – and she knew the writer's name, and that it starred Robert de Niro and that it was directed by Martin Scorcese. And I found out that she wants to go to university to study film making. How cool is that? I'm already wondering if we could work it out so that we go to the same university, even though I know that's stupid. Anyway, it wasn't all highbrow film talk; we did fool around a little too and that was great, except that I was constantly scared that her mum would just walk in on us. Rebecca wasn't scared though.

When I left at ten, Rebecca's mum still wasn't home. To tell the truth, I didn't want to leave, but Catherine was due home at any time, and I wanted to be there to talk to her. And when I did get home, Catherine was already there. So we were all of us sitting around and eating and talking with the TV on in the background for a couple of hours. And then Mum and Dad went to bed. And it was gone one o'clock before Sean went to bed, and then me and Catherine stayed up until about three.

In many ways, it was just like old times with me grilling her about university life in general and about life in Brighton more specifically. I can't get enough of Brighton and I love hearing her talk about the cafes and bars she goes to with her friends. I wonder sometimes whether she makes it sound more exotic and bohemian than it actually is, because she knows how much it thrills me to think of it being like that.

Some things we didn't speak about though. We didn't talk about Uncle Jack and Aunty Margaret. And we sure as hell didn't talk about the Ruger P95 lying hidden in a plastic bag under my bed.

Shit, the Ruger. I feel quite heavy with sadness at the thought of it as everything rushes back to me. Damn, and I was feeling so good, too. I've got to meet up with Sammy Williams and hand the Ruger over to him this afternoon. And I don't want to do it. I really don't want to hand it over. For a few stupid moments all kinds of ridiculous thoughts come to mind. Thankfully, I'm smart enough to throw them into the mental rubbish bin where they belong. I mean, do you see me pulling the Ruger on Sammy and telling him that it's mine now and that he can't have it back? No, me neither. How long would it be before I'm stabbed in the street, or shot dead or something like that? And it's not even Sammy's gun, is it? It belongs to someone even more dangerous than Sammy. Shit, it doesn't bear thinking about. Of course I'm going to give it back. Fact is, I'm *not* Travis Bickle. What the fuck do I want with a gun? The reminder of what I really want is downstairs with Mum. Catherine. University. A way out of here. A way, if I'm honest, out of a life where guns and crime and lawless behaviour feature at all. What have I been thinking? What has that fucking gun been doing to me? And when I think of it like that, all I can say is that getting rid of the stupid thing can't come soon enough. I feel better already. Time for a shower and time to get dressed.

Downstairs, Mum already has breakfast waiting for me. She's heard me in the shower. I'm the last one up, of course. Even Sean has been up and has eaten before retiring to his room like the anti-social troll that he is. Dad has gone to work; it's only half a day and he'll be back by three o'clock, but his firm is so busy that overtime like this has almost become compulsory. He moans about it, but I know that in a way he's pleased to have the money coming in.

I sit in the living room to eat my breakfast, served on a tray on my knee. Catherine and Mum are there too, and the telly is on in the background as ever.

'So, are we going out tonight then?'

As it happens, I'm free on Saturday; Rebecca and I are getting together on Sunday night. But I can't answer right away – I have to hastily chew and swallow before I can reply and I swear that Catherine has waited until I have a mouthful before she's asked me this. The way she's grinning at me as I try to force the bacon down my throat pretty much confirms it.

'Sure. I'm not doing anything.'

I try to make it sound pretty casual, but we both know that I love going out with Catherine.

'What, not seeing your little girlfriend on a Saturday night?'

Well no, I'm not actually. Rebecca already has plans. It will take a little while for our schedules to synchronise I guess. I don't say all this of course; I just shake my head to say no.

'OK, so where shall we go?'

I know that she's teasing – she knows that I don't go out bar-hopping all the time, like some my age.

'Why don't you decide?'

'I'll have a think. We'll decide later.'

And so we sit there talking and reading the papers and stuff, and it's really nice and I almost feel like this is a perfect world. Until I look at the clock and I have to remember the Ruger. No point delaying things; I have to get this sorted and the sooner the better.

I tell Mum and Catherine that I have to pop around to Andy's to return some books that I've borrowed from him and that he needs for a homework assignment. I don't even think they're still listening by the time I've finished explaining, which is good. I'm not going to be long.

Out on the streets, there's quite a breeze, and it's dark and grey with low cloud, but it's dry. There are people about, some in driveways washing their cars almost to spite the cold, others looking like they are going to or coming from some shopping expedition or other. Typical Saturday stuff and no mistake. There are also kids out playing; skateboards, bikes, doing whatever it is they are doing. I don't take much interest.

I have my black cotton jacket on, zipped up against the breeze. Under my arm I have a plastic bag and wrapped in it is the Ruger P95. I've wiped it very carefully all over so that I won't have left a trace of my having ever been in contact with it. Well, you can't be too careful, and I've watched enough *CSI* to know what to do.

As I walk through the streets of this familiar estate towards the line of shops on the perimeter, I'm feeling reluctant to hand over the gun again. Why can't I keep it? I keep getting the stupid scenarios running through my head again; me pulling the gun on Sammy, challenging him to take it from me if he wants it. Stuff like that. I have to try to remember where my real future lies. University. Brighton. Out of here. Best all round if the gun is just gone. I know only too well that if ever I was to use it, I would lose everything. It's that simple. So of course I'm just going to hand it over. It's a no-brainer. All the same, I feel like I'm being forced to do something I'd rather not do. It nags at me.

I'm walking along one of the rougher streets of the estate, the quickest way to where I'm headed. There's nobody on this street out washing cars on the driveway. No children out playing. A couple of the houses that I pass are boarded up. One of them is charred from a fire that ran through it. About a third of the houses in this street are empty and decaying. One house over on the far side of the street from where I'm walking has all the windows covered with wire mesh and a steel plate covering the front door. But this is not an abandoned house. Rumour has it that this is a house where a nasty criminal element runs its business. And that business is drug related of course. How true that is I can't honestly say, but rumours like that on an estate like ours are ones that you can pretty much believe. Certainly, I believe. I'm going to walk on by pretty quickly. This is not a place to dwell, not even when you're carrying a Ruger P95.

As I approach this locked up house, a kid looking a little too big for the BMX he's riding comes around the corner of an adjacent street. I can't see who this kid is because he's wearing a dark blue hoodie with the hood pulled right up. He looks up briefly and sees me though. And he stops and he points his hand right at me, and imitates a gun with his fingers and mimics firing a shot.

This chills and sickens me all at the same time. I'm scared, I don't mind saying. This kid then wheels his bike into the overgrown garden of the crime-house I've just been describing. I'm scared like I haven't been since before I started carrying the Ruger. I'm sure as hell not Travis Bickle right now and I'm cursing that Roddy Thompson ever forced me to look after his damned gun.

I'm past that house and around the corner onto a different street, quicker than you can imagine. I walk as fast as I can without running. But I'm not going faster than a bike. And it's a bike that whizzes past me, the same bike that I'd seen on the street I've just come from. And it's the same kid riding the bike. The kid passes me on the other side of the road and he reaches out his arm without looking and he's pointing something at me. Shit it's a gun!

I cry out and force myself back into the privet hedge that bounds the garden of the house I'm walking past. I hear a loud crack and I cry out again as I feel something hit my chest. It stings even through my cotton jacket and I look down fearing the worst and I'm almost weeping. But all I see is a silvery metal blob on the ground by my feet. I pick it up and inspect it. An air gun pellet. It was just an air gun. Well, yes, of course I'm relieved, but I'm also shaking with fear. And I can't help thinking what Sean told me and what Sammy told me; that word was going around that I was carrying a gun.

The kid on the bike has stopped at the end of the road. He's still sitting on his bike, arms folded and facing me as I approach on the opposite pavement. I can't help but look over as I pass, and I see the face beneath the hood now, grinning at me. It's the kid who had tried to mug me the other night. The kid I'd robbed at gun point. Oh fuck, what have I got myself into?

I hurry on by. The sooner I get to the shops and hand the sodding gun back to

Sammy Williams the better. I'm promising myself I'll work hard at school, that I'll get myself out, like it's a bloody mantra or something. I'm still saying this when I round a final corner and I see the police cars. Both exits to the alley behind the shops are blocked with police cars, blue lights flashing, the whole works. Well this is just great, isn't it? This is just what I need.

There are a few people – kids mostly – milling around trying to see what's going on, but Community Support Officers, those part-time ass-wipe pretend cops in their day-glo jackets, are keeping them back. I get as near as I can, conscious of what I'm carrying in the bag under my arm, but I'm trying to see if I can spot Sammy anywhere. Needless to say, I can't. Damn damn damn!

Then there's a bit of activity. I can see some cops coming out of the alley, quite a few of them. And they're escorting three kids and I know who these kids are; it's Sammy Williams and the two older boys I'd seen him with outside the school and at the Concrete Canyon. They've all got their hands behind their backs so they've been cuffed. Just before they push him into the car, Sammy Williams looks up and he sees me, and it's like I can see something click inside his head.

'You're dead, Davies. Dead. Fucking dead, you grass!'

It's all he can manage to shout before the cops shove him roughly into the back of one of their cars. Those two other boys from over on the Canyon say nothing as they are pushed into the backs of other cars. They don't have to. The way they're looking at me says enough. That's when I nearly faint, when I realise that Sammy was aiming his invective at me. Oh shit no, he can't believe that, he can't! I haven't grassed him up, I haven't. I wouldn't dare! But that's what he thinks. And that's what everyone will think now. Word's going to spread like wildfire. Oh God I'm dead. I'm dead. I'm dead.

Paramilitary social workers

I'm still holding the sodding Ruger, wrapped in its plastic bag as I get home. Only Sean is there. I pretty much ignore him even though he tries to say something to me. I just rush upstairs and hide the Ruger under my bed.

I'm slow coming back down the stairs, and Sean is still there, like he's been waiting for me.

'Where's Catherine? And Mum?'

'That's what I was trying to tell you.

They're over at Uncle Jack and Aunty Margaret's.'

Suddenly I feel cold, even though it's warm in the house.

'What's happened?'

'Somebody's been having a go at them. Messed the house up. I saw it when I went past this morning. Mum and Catherine have gone over to help them clean it up.'

Somebody. Well I have a bloody good idea who *somebody* is, and there's an itch at the back of my mind that can be scratched by fetching the Ruger from under my bed. I don't do that of course.

'Come on, let's go over.'

Sean doesn't need any encouragement, and pretty soon we're walking at some pace through the breeze towards Uncle Jack and Aunty Margaret's house.

I can pretty much guess what's

happened, but I still get Sean to give me the details as we walk. Sometime in the night, grey gloss paint has been thrown over the walls and windows of Uncle Jack and Aunty Margaret's house. Everything in the garden has been pulled up and thrown about, and there's even paint on the lawn. And someone has been pissing in through their letter-box and they've also been shoving paper bags full of human shit through the letter-box too. And there's shit smeared all over the front door.

Now I'm guessing that unless you actually live on an estate like ours you're pretty shocked by that. But let me tell you, it doesn't shock any of us. It sickens us, but it doesn't surprise us. That's just the sort of behaviour we've come to expect from the feral brutish louts that live among us. And there's absolutely nothing we can do about it. Not in the short term. Every now and then, you read in the papers about how a community has come together to gather evidence against a problem family, and eventually that family has been evicted and forced to move on. But the fact that these stories make the papers at all just shows how uncommon these little victories are. And the fact that you don't hear about them often shows how difficult it is to get that to happen. The worst thing is that when you really read these stories, it strikes you that the community has had to gather evidence for months and months. But in the meantime, decent people still have to suffer. People like Uncle Jack and Aunty Margaret.

When we get to the house, I see that Catherine is standing on some steps, scraping grey paint off the front windows. The paint seems to be coming away easily enough, but that does not make me feel better. In the garden, Mum is helping Uncle Jack gather up the torn-out plants and shrubs and sweep loose soil from the lawn and back into the trampled borders. I no longer feel like crying, not even when I see Uncle Jack looking so utterly broken. I just feel cold. And angry.

'Where's Aunty Margaret?'

I guess I'm worried because I don't see her.

Mum looks up from where she's crouched down, gathering together some undamaged green plants.

'She's inside, making some tea.'

Mum looks bewildered, like she can't believe anyone would behave like this. She should know better; she's lived on this estate all of her life. She's seen what it's become.

I take a moment to gather my thoughts. Right now I would gladly see the entire Rogers family killed.

'Has anyone called the police?'

Sean is right. The police should be here.

'As soon as we got here, about half an hour ago.'

Catherine will have called them herself. It's good that she's here.

'So where are they?'

I can hear the anger in Sean's voice and I know that it won't help.

'You know what it's like. They'll get here when they can be bothered and not before. Go and make sure Aunty Margaret's alright will you?'

Shit, but we shouldn't have to live like this, in fear of scum like the Rogers family. But it's just the way things are and there's nothing we can do about it.

Down the street I see two kids in hooded sweatshirts riding BMX bikes. It makes me think of the kid who had shot me with the air pistol earlier. That kid had gone into the fortified house on that rough street before he'd shot at me. A lot of kids like that are used to distribute drugs and crap. They are at the bottom of the food chain sure enough, but some of them will be looking to move up that career ladder. I wonder how many of them aspire to be squalid drug lords, controlling territories like the Concrete

Canyon, or estates like this one. I'd rather be dead than have nothing more than that to look forward to. I watch the kids on the bikes for a moment, long enough to see them approach a group of kids who are hanging out on a street corner. I can't see from this distance whether or not any trivial business is transacted, but I'm guessing that it is. It's the way things happen around here.

We clean and tidy the house and garden as best we can, leaving thick cardboard over the soiled hall carpet just behind the front door. As soon as we can, we'll get Dad to seal up that letter-box, and put a new and more secure one, with a tough spring-loaded flap, higher up in the door. Aunty Margaret just can't seem to stop crying, and who can blame her? And Uncle Jack just goes from bewilderment to anger, to sorrow, around and around until it becomes predictable. It's almost impossible to console them, but we all of us sit in that living room, as often as not in silence, until the police have come and gone. We have to wait more than two hours.

Well of course the police were all gushing

sympathy, but you could tell that right from the start they weren't really interested in doing anything. We all knew that the Rogers kids had done the damage, and Uncle Jack had even seen one of them standing and laughing in the street as he had opened the front door first thing this morning. But the police couldn't and wouldn't do more than take statements. That's all they can do, is what they told us. There isn't any evidence. And the upshot of it is that they are not even going to talk to the Rogers family. They're not going to make any attempt to warn those bastards off. But if it was to happen again and we were able to gather evidence, then they'd be more than happy to intervene. I like that word, intervene, don't you? Makes the police sound like mediators between criminals and victims, and not taking sides. That makes you feel safe, doesn't it? It makes me think about how the police are described by a journalist who writes for one of the Sunday papers; paramilitary social workers is what he calls them. I've never really understood what he meant by that. Until now. And do you know what their advice is? You couldn't make this up. Their best suggestion is for Uncle Jack and Aunty Margaret to get CCTV installed, like that's the answer to everything. Well I guess it does save them having to do their job.

When we finally come to leave Uncle Jack and Aunty Margaret's place, long after the police have gone, I am past being angry. I think that all of us are in shock. It's late as we open the front door. Uncle Jack is seeing us out, but Aunty Margaret can't face coming to the door. As we stand on the steps outside, saying our subdued goodbyes, I notice Derek Rogers and a couple of his goblins standing across the road, watching us. You can just see the smirking untouchable arrogance of the little bastard and I want to kill him right there where he stands.

'We're only going to come back and do it again.'

Laughing. Untouchable. And they know it. They can roam wild, commit any crime. No one dares come out as a witness. Just one family, and because of the unwilling impotence of the police, these are their streets and they can do as they like in them.

'Wanna bet?'

It's all too much for Sean. He's down the path and vaulting the gate even as I'm calling him back. The Rogers kid turns and runs but Sean is quite the athlete and catches him quickly, throwing him against a metal lamp post. I'm running after Sean, hoping that he doesn't lay into the Rogers kid.

'You're gonna stay away, or I'll kill you.'

Sean says something like that – I can't hear properly over my own breathing and my running footsteps – then throws the disgusting brat to the ground, where he inadvertently rolls in dog shit.

I take hold of Sean and lead him away, back to where Mum and Catherine are waiting for us down the road. I don't blame Sean, but I can't help thinking that our house could well be next now. I can hear all the foul language and threats but I'm beyond paying them any attention. What's done is done and we'll just have to live with it.

We catch up to Mum and Catherine – well actually, they're waiting for us – and we head for home with heavy hearts. We're walking mostly in silence and it feels like the grey clouds and even the twilight air are closing in on us. And then suddenly, Catherine cries out. Her hands go up to the back of her head and she drops to the ground. She's been hit on the back of the head by a huge rock, and as she lies there, moaning, we see the blood flooding from between her fingers. Behind us, we can see Derek Rogers and his friends running away fast, and I catch hold of Sean's arm to stop him from following them. There's a massive gash on the back of Catherine's head, and I tell Sean to use his phone to call an ambulance as Catherine slips into unconsciousness. It's all starting to get out of hand and there's no one who can or will help us.

It's late when we get home. The ambulance had come speedily enough, and thankfully, Catherine is OK. She regained consciousness quickly, but there was a huge flap of skin hanging off the back of her head and there was so much blood that all of us were scared. The paramedics managed to stem that and put a pressure pad over the wound, held in place by bandages. We arrived at the hospital Accident and Emergency unit within half an hour of the attack but we had to wait for two hours before anyone saw Catherine. The staff seemed overwhelmed but it didn't stop us feeling helpless and concerned.

While we were waiting, the police came and took a statement from us. We identified Derek Rogers, but after they left, I can't say I felt confident that anything would be done. Mum was crying a bit, and Catherine was pretty groggy and subdued and obviously in a great deal of pain. Eventually, she saw a doctor and her wound was stitched up and a huge bandage was wound around her head. Sean had called Dad, and he came to bring us all home.

As we are walking up the path to our front door, I am in front, and I see it first. The word 'grass' has been written in paint, in big letters over the door. My legs almost fail me when I see it. I feel sick. The words that Sammy Williams shouted at me as he was forced into the police car earlier in the day ring in my ears. I'd forgotten about all that. I'd forgotten all about the bloody Ruger. Oh fuck, what is happening to us? What have I done?

CHAPTER 18
Gun dog

It's early on Sunday morning and I'm the only one up and about. Actually, I haven't been to bed at all. I'm thinking that we are all in trouble. Mum, Dad, Sean, me. Perhaps not Catherine; she already has a bolt-hole to run to. She has Brighton and university. But the rest of us – just where can we run?

Dad was going spare all night and he called the police about the paint on our door, but they are not sending anyone out. There's nothing they can do anyway. And when they asked him if he'd like them to get someone from victim support to contact him, he nearly exploded with frustrated rage and slammed the phone down.

I find myself constantly looking out the front windows. I think that maybe I'm looking out for the next attack. I should have got rid of the gun earlier. I should have found Sammy and given it to him as soon as I'd known about Big Roddy being killed. At least we wouldn't be targeted for being grasses. I keep thinking of the kind of people that run the Concrete Canyon, and even the fortified house in that street not so far from here on this very estate. There can be no reasoning with people like that and no protection from the police. No one can look out for us twenty-four hours a day. I'm really scared. And that's before I think about what the feral Rogers family might have in store for us now.

Looking out of the window I see our neighbour, Alan, striding up his garden path, the two spaniels obediently following him. Gun dogs. I'm thinking about how I'd told myself that I was a gun dog when I was carrying the Ruger. Stupid to think that way, I reckon now. I hate that stupid gun now. I watch Alan usher the dogs into the back of his car, I watch him slide his shotgun in beside them. I watch as he pulls out into the road and silently glides away without a care in the world. Well that's OK; I feel that I have cares enough for all of us.

In the afternoon, we're all sitting around with the television on, but I don't think any of us are really watching it. We've been a quiet house, and Catherine has stayed in bed until really late. She slept in my room – which used to be her room. It makes me sick to see her head all wrapped up in that bandage. Even Dad is pretty subdued and I get the feeling that he's staying quiet for the sake of Mum and Catherine and all of us really. But I know he feels like he ought to be out there knocking somebody's head in. He's talked about going round to the Rogers' house, but we've managed to talk him out of it. I think he feels that he should be doing something for Catherine – and to a lesser degree, perhaps, Uncle Jack and Aunty Margaret. But Dad is a true family man and he understands that his responsibility to us means that he has to control his instinct for revenge. He probably doesn't use those words to himself, but that is what's happening. The way we're all sitting here, none of us wanting to talk much, and none of us going out, I feel like we're prisoners. Prisoners in our own home.

I've called Rebecca to call off our date for tonight. We need to stay together as a family and I just can't go out and try to enjoy myself the way things are. Actually, Rebecca was really wonderful about it. She was mortified to hear what had happened to Uncle Jack and Aunty Margaret and to Catherine. She was so understanding and she even offered to come around and spend an evening with us, but I told her that it would be best to do that another time. I feel like we are under siege.

It's about seven o'clock when the knock comes at the door. I answer it and it's the police, two of them, a man and a woman. I think that they've come to talk about what happened to Catherine, or about the vandalising of our front door. But when they come into the living room, what they tell us rocks us all to the core. Uncle Jack and Aunty Margaret have been found dead in their living room. It's pretty obvious that they couldn't come to terms with what had been happening to them over the last few days. And this lovely old couple, who had lived here their whole lives, found themselves unable to bear living with what this place had become. They'd swallowed a bottle of pills apiece and had found a final peace in each other's arms. I'm not going to describe our reaction to this news; you can paint your own picture.

Now, in the early hours of the morning, I'm a gun dog once again and I'm out on the streets with the Ruger in my pocket and I'm feeling that enough is enough. I'm approaching the Rogers' house.

I'm carrying a can of petrol, one we keep in the shed to fill the lawnmower. And I have some rags and a cigarette lighter. I'm pretty clear about what I'm going to do. I'm going to burn that bloody house out. Then the stinking Rogers bastards will have to move out. I can only hope that they're re-housed in the Concrete Canyon, where they belong. Enough is enough.

Up at the front door and it's eerily quiet. I soak the rags I'm carrying in petrol and then I pour the rest of the petrol in through their letter-box. God but there's a lot of it. Strangely, I don't feel the least bit tense or worried. I'm carrying all the protection I need in my pocket. Ruger P95 9mm semi-automatic centre-fire with twelve rounds in the magazine.

I set fire to the petrol-soaked rags and hastily shove them in through the letter-box. It all goes up quicker than I'd expected. I retreat to the far side of the road and I watch for a while until I see the whole front door go up in yellow flames. It's a lot fiercer and a lot quicker than I'd expected. I look up and I see one of the hated Rogers family looking down at me from an upstairs window and, for the first time, it occurs to me that they might all be trapped upstairs. They might die. And honestly, I don't feel a thing about that.

It turns out that the Rogers family survived the blaze. Some of them anyway. I'm at home, wishing like crazy that I hadn't done what I did. Two of the Rogers clan are battering at our front door. A brick has come through our front window. There's screaming and foul language.

Dad is shouting from upstairs, and Sean is yelling, asking what's going on. Dad will be dressed soon, and coming downstairs. And there is Catherine and Mum to consider. This is a problem of my making so it's up to me to sort it out.

I throw the front door open and there is the brutish Rogers father, ten feet away, contorted with rage and holding a huge piece of wood. The Ruger is out of my pocket faster than even I could imagine it. Fourteen pounds of pressure on the trigger cocks the hammer and fires the first round.

The big bastard goes down, a big hole blown in his thigh. And suddenly the whole street is quiet. There are neighbours all around, just staring, and this monster rolling on the floor and bleeding and his eldest son just staring at the gun in my hand. Not so tough now are you, you bottom-feeding mouth-breathing pig is all I'm thinking.

Behind me I can sense my dad and Sean, but I don't turn to face them. The only thought that's running through my mind is that I won't be going to Brighton now and I almost laugh at the absurdity. That's the least of my problems. I'm never going to escape this place the way that Catherine did. This place must have been too much a part of me all along. I am a product of this miserable environment and it's only now, too late, that I realise it.

It must only be moments and the silence is broken, not with a bang, but with the gradually approaching sirens of police cars. I'm conscious of the gun still held loose in my right hand, and I can see the flashing of the blue lights down the road long before

I see the cars themselves. They're here now though, quick enough. Nowhere to be seen when Uncle Jack and Aunty Margaret needed them, but they'll go out of their way to deal with a mad dog. And that's just what I am now, I suppose; a mad dog. A gun dog.